CHILLED TO THE DOG BONE

---

a Samantha Davies mystery

S.A. Kazlo

For Rita Bolster for your kindness and support.

WINGS FALLS

A. SWEETIE PIE'S CAFÉ
B. THE CLOTHES HORSE
C. THE SMILING PIG
D. THE SOUND MACHINE
E. THE TOY BOX
F. SAINT ANTHONY'S CATHOLIC CHURCH
G. CIVIL WAR MONUMENT
H. THE EWE AND ME WOOLERY
I. MOMMA MIA'S
J. THE NUT HOUSE
K. WINGS FALLS LIBRARY
L. WINGS FALLS PARK
M. AL'S FLY SHOP
N. TOP DRAWER CONSIGNMENTS
O. CANDIE PARKER- HOGAN'S HOME
P. WINGS FALLS SENIOR CENTER
Q. WINGS FALLS POLICE STATION
R. WINGS FALL COMMUNITY COLLEGE
S. SHOP AND SAVE
T. SAMANTHA DAVIES' HOME
U. WINGS FALLS ANIMAL HOSPITAL

Acknowledgements

A huge thank you to my Thursday night GFWG. Without you this wouldn't happen.

Thank you to my publisher Gemma Halliday for making my dreams come true. A big kiss from Porkchop, too.

Thank you to Jennifer Rarden for whipping my scribbles into shape.

And for my biggest cheerleader and believing in me, my husband, Michael, I love you.

My readers, thank you from the bottom of my heart for taking the time to enter my little world of Wings Falls and its characters.

CHAPTER ONE

———

"How do I look? Should I wear a crown?" Gladys O'Malley, the senior member of my rug hooking group, the Loopy Ladies, sat on her "throne" in the outhouse we were sponsoring. The outhouse race would take place on Sunday morning. This weekend, the Firemen's Convention was being held at the Civic Center in Lake George, a resort town in upstate New York. My local fire company, Wings Falls Fire Department, was the host. It was held annually as close to Saint Patrick's Day as possible. Fun and green beer abounded. All the local fire companies who attended entered a homemade outhouse, decorated by a local group, like the Loopy Ladies, who'd volunteered to sponsor this year's outhouse for our hometown fire company. We often lent our services and talents to worthy causes. This past fall, we sold small rugs we hooked to raise money for Camp Adirondack, a summer camp that invites kids from the inner city for two weeks of fun in the fresh mountain air.

I stomped my feet. Even though I wore my warmest fleece-lined boots and a pair of heavy wool socks, cold seeped through from the cement floor of my garage. A space heater blasted out warm air but barely made a dent in the freezing March air flowing into the drafty garage. I glanced at my cousin, Candie, and noticed her tugging a purple wool cap over her ears to stave off the cold air. I envied my dachshund, Porkchop, Candie's calico cat, Dixie, and the newest member of her family, Annie, a small dog of indeterminate breed, snuggled on the rug next to the fireplace in my living room.

Helen Garber poked at the bright-orange glasses sliding down her nose. "Haul your skinny old butt out of there and help us finish hanging the rugs we hooked on the wall of the outhouse, so we can get out of this blooming cold."

I rolled my eyes towards the rafters of my garage. Leave it to Helen to pick a fight with Gladys. She was the most outspoken member of the group. Her tongue knew no boundaries. She often said she "told it like it is." Not only did her tongue know no boundaries, but neither did her wardrobe choice. The louder and bolder the color, the better. Today her ample figure sported a lemon yellow jacket she paired with hot pink pull-on polyester slacks.

I walked over to the outhouse and admired our handiwork. We had painted green shamrocks over a white background in honor of Saint Patrick's Day on the outside walls.

Candie stood next to me. "Not a bad painting job, don't y'all think?"

I smiled. My cousin had moved north over fifteen years ago from Hainted Holler, Tennessee, and you could still cut her thick southern accent with a knife.

"We Loopy Ladies are a multi-talented group. Not only can we hook with the best of them, but we wield a mean paintbrush, too." I turned to the six of us who were gathered in my garage. "Don't you agree, ladies? Our outhouse will leave the others in the dust."

Cheers erupted from my fellow hookers. There are usually twelve of us who gather every Monday morning at our friend Lucy Foster's rug hooking studio. Although our absent members were busy elsewhere, everyone had contributed a rug to decorate the outhouse.

Susan Mayfield clapped her hands to get our attention. "We'd better finish hanging our rugs. Hank, Mark, and Brian will be here shortly to lift the outhouse onto the back of Brian's truck. They need to drive it to the staging area for the race on Sunday morning."

Susan and her husband, Brian, own Momma Mia's, which I believe is the best Italian restaurant this side of the Big Apple. Brian had volunteered his truck for transporting our outhouse to the race's starting area, a park next to the Civic Center. The racecourse was covered with snow and groomed to perfection for the outhouses. Hank Johnson, my boyfriend, and Mark Hogan, Candie's newly minted husband, were going to help provide the brawn to lift the outhouse on and off the truck. There were official rules for the race. The outhouse had to weigh two-hundred-and-fifty pounds and measure four feet wide by five feet tall. Once at the park, the fellows would attach skis to the bottom of the outhouse to help it move smoothly across the snow. Every outhouse had to have a rider, and this year, we had nominated Gladys for the honor.

"Need a hand up?" I asked Gladys as she tottered a bit when she tried to push off the wood board that served as the seat in the outhouse—or, as she liked to call it, her throne.

Gladys patted her green-dyed curls. She changed the color of her hair to match a season or event—orange for the fall, red for Valentine's Day. Last summer she even dyed her hair violet to coordinate with the color scheme of Candie's wedding.

Gladys pushed away the hand I offered her for assistance. "What do you think I am, an old lady?" She rose and exited the outhouse.

I heard chuckles as she joined the rest of us, and I swear Helen said, "Yeah, older than dirt," under her breath.

Jane Burrows picked up the stack of small rugs we needed to attach to the inside walls of the outhouse. "Let's see what we have and where to hang them." Ever the organized one, she was our town's librarian, but she also had a vested interest in the convention since her boyfriend, Jim Turner, was the chief of our town's fire company. Like me, Jane had found true love late in life, although I didn't feel the midfifties as being all that old. She had lived most of her life with her mother. Me, I was divorced after being married for twenty-five years. I discovered my ex doing the late-night bump fuzzies with the secretary of the funeral parlor we co-own, the Do Drop Inn Funeral Parlor.

Jane spread the rugs out on a folding table I'd set up in the corner of my garage. Our theme for this project was to hook something that meant a lot to us. We gathered around the table to admire the finished rugs. I had hooked a rug featuring my Porkchop curled up hugging his favorite hedgehog squeaky toy.

A smile curved my lips as my eyes traveled over the rugs spread before me. "Anita, how appropriate. The ruler and the letters A, B, C really capture what you do." Anita Plum was often a substitute teacher at our local high school.

Her blonde ponytail swayed back and forth as she groaned. "My original thought was to hook a large bottle of aspirin, what with my girls and their teenage antics." Anita's twin teenage girls, Sara and Susie, kept her on her toes. While my ex and I had never had children, I didn't envy Anita raising teenagers in today's world. In my opinion, she deserved a medal.

Next, I ran my fingers over Susan Mayfield's rug. My mouth started to water at the plate of spaghetti she had hooked. "Susan, I can practically taste Brian's delicious pasta and sauce."

Susan laughed. "If I'm not hooking, taking care of my two little ones, Robby and Molly, you'll find me at the restaurant, so I thought spaghetti was a pretty large part of my life."

Candie flicked back behind her ear a strand of auburn hair that escaped her hat. "Yes, and a delicious part."

Susan ran a slim hand through her short, frosted hair. "I won't argue with you on that one. Brian does know how to prepare a mean bowl of spaghetti."

Heads nodded around the table in agreement.

Next in line on the table was Candie's rug, a cluster of five gold rings, but not just any rings. Each was set with a large gemstone. I've often said my cousin's middle name was bling. I glanced over at her hands. Yep, each finger had a large gemstone ring on it, except the ring finger of her left hand, which wore a modest gold wedding band and engagement ring. It might have taken Candie eleven engagements, but she finally found Mr. Right in Mark, Wings Falls mayor.

The rugs scattered on the table were all hooked with love and represented a fine group of ladies.

I pointed to Jane Burrows' rug, an open book. "It must have been a difficult decision, Jane, whether to make a rug about your career as a librarian or your involvement with the fire company."

Jane blushed. After living with her mother as a single woman for her whole life, having a love interest was a new experience for her. "Oh, a book was a lot easier than hooking a fire engine. Maybe next year, if Jim is still fire chief."

CHAPTER TWO

———

My eyes widened in shock at Jane's statement. "What do you mean *if* Jim's still fire chief? Is he planning on retiring or moving out of the area?"

Jane shrugged and fidgeted with the edge of her rug. "Umm, nothing. I don't know what I was saying. How about we tack the rugs to the inside of the outhouse. Like you said, the guys will be here soon to load it onto Brian's truck." Jane picked up her rug and walked towards the outhouse.

I turned to Candie. "Has Mark mentioned anything about Jim leaving the fire company?"

Candie's hair swung about her shoulders as she shook her head. "No, he hasn't said a word to me about Jim or his leaving the fire company, and I haven't heard anything at the office, either." Candie worked as Mark's part-time secretary. Wings Falls was a small community and didn't have the budget for a full-time position. The arrangement suited Candie fine, as my cousin's main passion, aside from Mark, was writing steamy romance novels.

"Hank hasn't said a thing to me, either. I wonder if Jim is planning a career change." While Jane and I hooked together, I didn't feel comfortable enough to ask her any further questions about Jim leaving. It would be a big loss for the town if he did. He'd been a member of the fire company for at least twenty-five years and its fire chief for eight of those years. He had done a lot to improve its services for Wings Falls. I shrugged. Maybe he wanted to retire. He was in his late fifties, so it seemed reasonable.

"Ladies, let's get this show on the road. I want our entry in the outhouse race to be the best looking. After all, I'll be sitting on the "throne", and I want it to show off all of my grandeur."

I about choked on my laughter. Leave it to Gladys to put things in perspective. She was the oldest Loopy Lady, and no one really knew her exact age, though I guess she was somewhere in her eighties. We'd voted her the honor of riding in the outhouse, but she'd taken it to the extreme. One would have thought she was the Queen of England and was going to ride in the royal carriage amongst her subjects.

I turned to Helen. She stood at the far end of the table biting her lower lip. Knowing her, probably to keep from letting a snarky comment escape.

The other ladies and I gathered up the rugs and brought them over to the outhouse. On the way, I grabbed a hammer and box of tacks from what had once been my father's workbench. I'd spent many an hour when I was growing up sitting on a stool watching him as he repaired something for my mother or hammered together one of the many birdhouses he used to make for our yard. He loved to watch and feed our feathered friends. After my divorce from George, my parents signed my childhood home, a brick ranch, over to me and moved to sunny Florida to enjoy evening cocktails with their friends Herb and Marge Feinstein. I missed them, but I understood why they wanted to enjoy the warm weather Florida had to offer as I glanced out the side window of my garage at the two feet of snow still covering my lawn in the middle of March.

I placed the hammer and box of tacks on a small table I had set up next to the outhouse. Since the race was an event sponsored by the fire company, we asked Jane to direct us as to where the small rugs should be hung.

Jane pointed to the pile of rugs. "We'll attach six rugs on one inside wall and the other six opposite it."

I stepped inside the outhouse and held out my hand for the first rug to tack to the wall.

"Here, hang mine first." Helen Garber handed me her rug, a large pair of bright orange eyeglasses hooked with a vibrant pink background. If nothing else, the loud colors she'd used in this rug would wake you up in the morning.

I grabbed up my hammer and plucked some tacks out of the box. I positioned the rug on the left wall of the outhouse.

I was about to affix it to the wall when Helen spoke up again. "No. No. Not there. No one will see it," she said. She pointed to the back wall of the outhouse. "There. I want it there. Place it over Gladys's head."

I did an eye roll and readjusted her rug over the seat where Gladys would be holding court on her ride to the finish line.

Helen nodded. "That's better."

Gladys patted her green curls with a gnarled hand. "*Humph.* The crowd will be looking at me and not your silly rug."

To avoid a verbal, knock-down fight, I quickly nailed the rug in place then reached for another. I was careful to place the tacks between the loops of the rugs so they wouldn't cause any damage to the wool strips or backing.

Hanging the remaining rugs went fairly quickly with no one else voicing any preference as to where their rug should be hung.

When my job was finished, I brushed back a strand of *very* curly brown hair that had fallen over my eyes and stepped back to admire my handiwork. "What do you think, ladies? Do we have a winner here or what?"

"A winner with a capital W," Cookie Harrington said. Cookie pulled a brown wool knit cap over her ears. The color was a close match to her smooth dark skin. She worked at the Wings Falls Animal Hospital as their receptionist and was the newest member of our group. Her skill as a rug hooker was growing in leaps and bounds. I believed with her, it was an inherited talent. At one of our Monday morning meetings at The Ewe, she mentioned her mother was a hooker and often won first prize at the county fair. I felt like, before long, Cookie would be doing the same.

I turned at the sound of a truck rumbling up my driveway. "Looks like the guys are ready to pick up our masterpiece."

A blast of wind blew into my garage as I opened the door. The space heater couldn't keep up with the cold that invaded our space.

Hank, Mark, and Brian climbed out of Brian's Ford truck and walked towards us. A smile spread across my face as my tall, dark, and handsome boyfriend approached me. He placed an arm around my shoulders and kissed the top of my head. "All finished?"

"Yep." I took his hand and led him over to the outhouse.

"Hmm, shamrocks. That certainly keeps with the theme of the weekend. But no mugs filled with green beer?"

I laughed and poked him in the side. His down vest softened my jab. "There'll be plenty of beer tomorrow night at the dance after all the activities planned for the day."

With her arm slipped through Mark's, Candie joined us.

"Did someone mention green beer?" Mark asked.

Candie wrinkled up her freckle-sprinkled nose. "Green beer? Yuck."

I laughed. "It's only a few drops of green food coloring added to the beer to make it look festive."

Candie batted her long eyelashes at her new husband. "I'd rather have a glass of green wine."

My cousin was the only woman I knew who could use that feminine ploy and not look silly.

"I'll get you whatever you want tomorrow night," Mark said, giving her hand a gentle squeeze.

"Ready to load this puppy onto my truck?" Brian asked. "The outhouse is pretty heavy. Let's move everything out of our way so we can back the truck into the garage closer to it. The outhouse will be easier to load." Brian ran a hand through his mop of wavy red hair. He was a large fellow. Not heavy, but muscular. I imagined lifting large pots of spaghetti all day in his restaurant was a good workout.

"Sounds like a plan," Hank and Mark said in unison. We all laughed but set to work helping to clean the area in front of the outhouse.

"I saw Brian's truck pull up. Can I be of any help?"

My head snapped around to see Frank Gilbert standing in the entrance of my garage. He was my next-door neighbor, but more importantly, he was Gladys O'Malley's significant other. She once mentioned he kept her toes warm on a cold winter's night, which I thought was TMI.

"Pookie Bear!" Gladys called out and ran to him. "My man of the hour. I'm sure these young men could use your muscle to load the outhouse onto Brian's truck." Gladys squeezed his bicep to prove her point.

"Hi, Frank, much appreciated. I think we're about to load this." Hank smiled his way.

"Come on. You young fellows should be able to lift the outhouse in one try. Pookie Bear, show those youngsters how it's done."

I glanced in the direction of the voice egging the men on and laughed at Gladys. She pumped the air with her scrawny arms, cheering for them. She was one of a kind. She was not only my neighbor but also Hank's aunt. A peeling fishing boat sat in her backyard. An urn with the ashes of her first husband, Captain Stan, sat at the decaying helm.

With a number of hefty grunts from the guys and cheers from the ladies, the outhouse was finally loaded onto Brian's truck. Hank jumped up onto the bed and secured it with straps for the ride into Lake George, where it would be stored until the race on Sunday morning.

The guys stood at the rear of the truck admiring their handiwork. "Would you all like a drink as a reward for your hard work?" I asked.

"I'll take a rain check. This bugger is heavy, and I think we need a clear head when we deliver it to the park." Hank turned to the other fellows, and they nodded their heads in agreement.

"Oh, one last thing." I walked over to a shelf that lined the garage and pulled down an old blanket. I grabbed the hammer and tacks we'd used for the rugs. "When you deliver the outhouse to the staging area, will you nail this blanket on the front? We don't want anyone to see what we've created before the race."

CHAPTER THREE

———

Mark held his hand out to me for the blanket, hammer, and tacks. I gasped when I saw the flaming red scratch on the back of his hand. I wondered if they were claw marks and if the wound was infected.

I turned to Candie, who stood by my side. "What happened to Mark's hand? Did he tangle with a bobcat and lose?"

Tears gathered on her long lashes. "No. It was Dixie."

My eyes flew open in surprise. "Dixie? But she loves Mark. You never had a problem with her before. Right?"

Candie swiped at her eyes and looked around the crowded garage. "I don't want to talk about it now. All I'll say is there's a big issue in the Parker-Hogan household."

I couldn't blame her for not wanting to say anything with all these ladies in close listening distance of what she would tell me. While they were all good friends, Wings Falls was a small town and gossip spread like wildfire.

I placed a comforting arm around my cousin's shoulder and gave her a hug. "After everyone leaves, we'll settle on my sofa with a glass of wine, and you can tell me all about it."

Tomorrow would be a day filled with four-wheeler, ice fishing, cornhole, and skillet toss contests. The Fireman's Ball held at the Civic Center in Lake George would top off the evening.

Hank, Mark, and Brian strode over to us and gave their respective ladies a farewell kiss.

"Frank, would you like to come with us? We could use the muscle in getting this off the truck, plus we still have to attach the skis to the bottom." Hank pointed to the bottom of the outhouse where the skis would go in order for it to travel smoothly over the snow during the race.

Frank's craggy face split into a wide grin. My sweet detective had made my neighbor's day by including him in with the other guys.

Frank raised a bushy eyebrow at Gladys. She waggled her fingers at him, waving him along with the other men. "You go ahead, Pookie. Show these boys how it's done."

Laughter echoed around the garage as Frank scooted over to Gladys, planted a kiss on her lined cheek, and then hurried to Brian's truck and hefted himself into the back seat.

We all waved as Brian drove down the driveway. He honked and headed down the road. I turned to the ladies and asked, "Would anyone like a cup of coffee or tea?"

"Thanks, but I'm pooped," and "I need to get home," answered me back from the Loopy Ladies.

The ladies helped to put away the tools we'd used in painting and hanging the rugs. I thanked them for their help and waved as they walked to their cars. They had parked on the road in front of my house in order to keep my drive free for when Brian arrived.

Gladys started towards my garage door.

"Gladys, where do you think you're going?" I asked.

She turned back towards me. Weariness settled on her face. It had been a long day for her. Heck, *I* was bushed. "Home to wait for my Pookie Bear."

I shook my head. "You wait right there. I'll get my car and drive you home."

"Don't be silly. I only live next door. I can manage."

"Silly would be you slipping on a patch of ice. Candie, make sure she doesn't go anywhere while I fetch the Bug." I reached into my pocket for the keys to my egg-yolk yellow VW Bug convertible. I dodged a few ice patches as I navigated my way down my drive. I shuddered to think of Gladys falling because she slipped on one of them.

Within minutes, I drove up my drive to a waiting Gladys. While she settled into my car, I called out the passenger window, "Candie. See to the pets then pour us both a glass of wine."

"Will do," she answered then stepped back from the car as I drove next door to Gladys's house.

* * *

Candie and I were ensconced on the chintz-covered sofa in my living room. A fire blazed in the fireplace across from us. Annie, Dixie, and Porkchop lay curled up on the rug in front of the fire doing what they love to do best, sleep. While Dixie tolerated Porkchop, she was devoted to Annie, rarely leaving her side.

I took a sip of Riesling from the glass Candie poured for me while I delivered Gladys to her front door. "Okay, spill it. What's going on with you and Mark?"

Candie stared at her wineglass as if it held the answers to the world's most important secrets. Tears started to trickle down her smooth cheeks.

I placed my wineglass on the wooden trunk in front of the sofa and scooted over to her. I took her glass from her hand and set it next to mine then gathered her into my arms. "Sweetie, what's the matter? You know you can tell me anything."

Candie's chest heaved with deep sobs.

CHAPTER FOUR

———

Candie raised her head, her usually sparkling with life violet eyes were bloodshot. Tears pooled on her long lashes. "Mark and I are going to have to live in separate homes."

The shock of her statement jerked me back on my sofa cushion. I would have sworn there were pots of gold at the end of a rainbow before believing what Candie just proclaimed. "What are you talking about? Mark loves you. Heck, he pursued you for five years until he finally broke down the one-date rule you imposed on fellows when you moved north."

Candie swiped at the tears rolling down her cheeks. A faint smile crossed her lips. "Yes, he did. After eleven failed engagements, protecting my heart was my main concern, but he won it anyway."

I leaned over to the trunk and grabbed our glasses of wine. "Here. Take a sip and tell me what this is all about." I handed a glass to her then settled back against my cushion, waiting for her to tell me what caused all this crying.

Candie cradled her glass in her hands. She sniffled then hiccupped. "Remember Cuddles and how much Dixie loved him, even though we only had him for a few days?"

I nodded and thought of the scruffy little bundle of fur who literally barreled into Candie's life last fall at the Taste of Wings Falls, a food and craft fair held every October in our town's park. The little fellow had escaped from a young family camping in the area. He was on his own for over a week and was desperate for food. In his hunt for something to eat, he had snatched Gladys's fanny pack that contained a smelly limburger and ham sandwich.

Candie nodded in agreement. "Yes, and Dixie fell in love with him. She was devastated when Cuddles's real owners contacted For Pet's Sake to claim him."

For Pet's Sake was Wings Falls's local animal shelter. They, along with our local newspaper, the *Tribune,* had featured pictures of

Cuddles on their websites. Fortunately, or unfortunately for Candie, a young family saw Cuddles's picture and contacted the shelter.

My forehead wrinkled in a frown. I still didn't understand what this all had to do with Mark and Candie living apart. "Yes, but Dixie loves Annie as much as she did Cuddles. What does this all have to do with Dixie scratching Mark and this nonsense about you living in separate homes?"

Candie slammed her glass of wine back down on the trunk. She stood, placed her hands on her hips, and glared down at me. "Don't you see? Mark was the one who took Cuddles from our home and to the pet shelter. Dixie won't let him near Annie. She's afraid the same thing will happen to the new love of her life."

Uh-oh. Candie was teetering on the edge of a duck fit, the Southern equivalent to having a pretty good mad on. I needed to defuse things before it got to the flying duck fit stage, or I'd have to dive for cover under my sofa.

I patted the sofa cushion. "Come on, sit down so we can discuss this."

Candie blew out a breath, ruffling her bangs, and plopped back down. "Last night, Dixie, Annie, and I were sitting on the sofa. Mark sat next to me and leaned in for a kiss. Dixie hissed then shot her paw out and scratched his hand.

"Oh, my. I imagine Mark wasn't too happy." Having experienced a cat scratch or two over the years, I knew they could sting.

"No, he wasn't. Cradling his hand, he marched off to the bathroom mumbling something about it was either the cat or him. Of course, I joined him in the bathroom and tended to his cut. Sam, what am I to do? I can't give up Dixie. I've been her momma forever. Maybe marriage is not meant for me. Look at my track record! Eleven failed engagements." Tears flowed from Candie's eyes again.

I reached over and squeezed her hand. "He didn't act mad earlier when he came to help pick up the outhouse."

Dixie left her bed by the fireplace and jumped onto the sofa. She curled up on Candie's lap. Candie idly stroked the cat's fur then raised her eyes to me. "He always calls me Sweetie or some sort of endearment. Did you hear any of those from him in your garage?"

Thinking back, I couldn't say I had. "No, but maybe it's because there were other ladies present. After all, he is the mayor of our town. Maybe he was going for some sort of decorum?"

Candie laughed. "Other people never stopped him before."

What she said was true. While Mark wasn't overly demonstrative in public, he did have his pet names for her.

"I'd better gather my fur children and head home. Maybe Mark will be there and we can talk about what's happening between him and Dixie."

I placed a hand over my mouth to cover a yawn that wanted to escape and pushed myself off the sofa. "Are you okay to drive home? You could always leave Precious here and have Mark come by and pick you up." Precious was Candie's '73, baby blue Mustang.

Candie shook her head. "No, I'm fine. I only took a couple sips of the wine. Talking things out with you was a big help."

Her words warmed my heart. I leaned over and hugged her. Dixie jumped to the floor as I invaded her space. "That's what families are for. I know Mark loves you with all of his heart and you'll work things out. Remember what Memaw Parker used to say." Memaw Parker was our grandmother and had raised Candie since she was five after her parents were killed in an automobile accident.

A smile spread across Candie's face. "We're Parkers and can do anything."

I squeezed Candie to my side. "That's right, and don't you forget it."

She laughed and pushed herself off of the sofa. "How can I, when you are constantly reminding me?"

She walked over to the snoozing dogs. A chill began to settle over the living room as the fire in the fireplace died down. Candie bent and gently rubbed the fur on Annie's back to awaken her. The waning firelight reflected off the rings adorning her fingers. "Annie, time to go home. Daddy will probably be waiting for us."

Her pets were definitely the children she never had and were loved just as much. "Come on, Annie. Let's put your sweater back on. It's cold outside." She slipped a pink knit sweater over Annie's small head. Candie grabbed a rhinestone-studded leash off the wing chair sitting next to the fireplace and clipped it onto Annie's collar. I smiled. My cousin had passed her love of bling on to her fur babies.

Porkchop raised his head to see what was happening then lowered it and began softly snoring again. I guess we were disturbing his beauty sleep.

Candie bent and scooped Dixie into her arms and walked towards my front door. I followed behind the mini family. When we got to my entrance, she turned and placed an arm around my shoulder and pulled me into a hug. "Thank you for being here for me and listening to all my woes." Dixie meowed and squirmed in Candie's arms.

"Oops. Sorry, Dixie." I pulled back and ruffled the fur between her ears then glanced over at Candie. "Things will work out. Dating a person and being married to them are two different ballgames. Mark loves you, I have no doubt. And I know you love him. Bat those fabulous eyelashes of yours at him and put your feminine wiles to work."

Candie laughed and fluttered the aforementioned eyelashes at me. "I do have a way with the opposite sex, don't I?"

I swatted at her arm. "Go on. We've got a big day tomorrow, and I need to get my beauty sleep."

I shivered as a blast of cold air swept into my house when the front door opened. After everyone left Candie moved her car up my driveway. I watched as she loaded Dixie and Annie in her car and waved as she drove away. She honked then drove off into the darkness.

I closed the door and retraced my steps to where Porkchop slumbered. "Porkchop, do you want to sleep there or join me in my bedroom?" Having received no answer, I left him to his dreams. I checked my phone for any messages from Hank. I'd had to purchase a new phone when my ever-trusty flip phone died after I'd forgotten to take it out of my jeans pocket while doing the wash. While I did't have the fanciest smart phone at least now I could text and download apps. I smiled when a text from him read *I love you* and a *Sweet dreams*.

Tomorrow was going to be a long and busy day. One I hoped went well for all of us.

CHAPTER FIVE

———

I stomped my feet to get the feeling back into them. Standing on frozen Lake George had chilled me to the bone, in spite of all the layering I had donned. I wore my fleece-lined boots and poofy winter coat, under which I wore a turtleneck and sweater. My jeans were lined with flannel, and a wool knit cap was pulled over my ears. My gloved hands were tucked under my armpits to keep them warm. I felt like the Michelin man times two. If someone bumped into me, I feared I'd topple over. Hank had picked me up at eight this morning. We dropped both his miniature bulldog, Nina, and my dachshund, Porkchop, off at For Pet's Sake for an overnight stay. Shirley Carrigan, the shelter's owner, had added doggie day care and boarding for added income to help support the shelter portion of For Pet's Sake. Her crew provided excellent care for our pups. We'd both be busy all day, and with the Fireman's Ball this evening, we wouldn't be home long enough to see to the pups' needs.

"Here, drink this. It should warm you up."

I smiled at the sound of the voice behind me. It belonged to the love of my life—well, the other love of my life besides Porkchop—Detective Hank Johnson. We'd met more than a year ago over a dead body. Newly transferred to the Wings Falls Police department from Albany PD, he wanted a quieter pace of life. He figured he'd find it in my small hometown of Wings Falls.

At six-foot, he looked down at my five-foot-four inches. I gazed up into his crystal-blue eyes and pushed back the dark-brown curl with a mind of its own that insisted on falling over his forehead.

"Thank you," I said and relieved him of the cup of hot apple cider he held out to me. I took a sip and groaned. "This is delicious and hits the spot. The warmth is sliding right down to my toes. It's starting to thaw them out."

Hank leaned in close and whispered into my ear, "There are better ways to warm you up."

Now heat flooded my whole body as I imagined what he had in mind. "Hold that thought until after the dance tonight."

Hank waggled his eyebrows at me. "Will do. I plan to take advantage of the dogs doing a sleepover at the shelter."

I laughed then felt a tug at my heart.

Hank lifted my chin with a gloved finger. "Why the sad face all of a sudden?"

I shrugged my shoulders. "I miss Porkchop. It's not often he's not home. I'm used to having my little guy around."

Hank drew me next to him. I snuggled into his down coat. "We'll pick them up before the outhouse race and spend the rest of the day giving the dogs our undivided attention. How's that sound? We'll even stop at the grocery store and buy a special rawhide bone for them on the way over to the shelter."

I smiled up at him. "You're the best. You know that? You knew the way to my heart was through Porkchop."

"Aww, you discovered my secret."

I poked him in the side with my free hand. "Come on, let's go check out the four-wheeler race. It should be starting soon. I believe Frank Gilbert is entered."

When I left Porkchop out to do his business this morning in my fenced-in backyard, I noticed Frank loading his four-wheeler onto the back of his pick-up truck. Gladys stood outside in her robe and fuzzy bunny slippers supervising. I called over good morning, and she mentioned Frank was on his way into Lake George for the race.

The roar of the four-wheeler engines grew louder as we approached the starting line. Helmeted riders sat on their vehicles and gunned their engines. A crowd gathered behind a rope separating them from the contestants. Gladys was front and center, pressed up against the rope. I grabbed Hank's arm with my free hand and clutched my half-finished cup of hot apple cider with the other. We edged our way to Gladys.

"Morning again, Gladys. I see Frank is ready for the race to begin."

Gladys's green curls bounced as she nodded. Green was her main color scheme today and, I bet, for most of the weekend. Along with her green curls, she wore a green wool scarf tied around her neck. The bottoms of her green slacks were tucked into socks decorated with leprechauns and shamrocks.

She pointed to the racer with the number seven pinned to the back of his jacket. "My Pookie Bear is going to win. I know he is."

"My fingers will be crossed for him," I said then took a sip of my drink.

A Wings Falls firefighter approached the starting line with a bullhorn clutched in his hand. Since the fire company sponsored the activities this weekend, they would man all the events. I had seen the young fellow at various fire company events but didn't know him personally, which wasn't unusual, as new members were frequently joining the fire company. He tossed the cigarette he had clamped in his lips on the ground and raised the bullhorn to his mouth. I wasn't going to pass judgement, not that I liked him littering. Who was I to judge? Smoking was such an addictive habit and especially in one so young. "Good morning. I'm Drew Ellis. How's everyone today?"

A chorus of *good morning*s and *fine*s answered him back.

"Thank you for joining us on this sunny Saint Patrick's Day weekend and for supporting your local fire company. Now, are the racers ready? If so, rev your engines."

I handed Hank my cup and placed my hands over my ears as a deafening sound of engines filled the air. Gladys pulled her green and white striped hat farther down her head.

Hank laughed at his aunt and me.

Drew lifted the bullhorn once again. "All right, folks, count down with me—ready, set...."

"*Go!*" shouted the gathered crowd.

Ten four-wheelers lurched forward on the ice and skidded around orange safety cones marking the racecourse.

The crowd cheered and shouted encouragement to their favorite racer. Gladys jumped and clapped her hands, yelling for her Pookie Bear to bring home first place. I smiled and slipped my hand through Hank's arm. I hoped my energy was as great as his aunt's when I approached her age.

After much slipping and sliding, the vehicles crossed the finish line. Unfortunately, Frank wasn't first. That honor went to a teenager who roared to first place inches in front of Frank.

Gladys turned to us and stuck out her lower lip. "My Pooks was robbed. That kid pulled in front of him. It has to be illegal. Hank, go arrest him."

Hank shook his head. "Aunt Gladys, this is a race on ice. There is nothing illegal about it. The teen won fair and square."

Gladys jutted out her jaw. "Humph. What good is it having a police officer in your family if they won't do anything for you?"

A helmeted figure walked towards us—Frank. He slipped off his head gear and ran a gloved hand through his grey hair, causing it to stand on end. Gladys shuffled up to him, mindful of the ice she walked on. Frank put an arm around her shoulder and dutifully nodded as she ranted on about how he had really won the race.

I took one last sip of my drink. "Your aunt isn't too happy with you right now."

He shrugged his shoulders. "She'll get over it. She'll vent for a while then be on to something else."

The new fireman, Drew, gave Hank a nod as he walked past us.

"He's new to the fire company. Do you know him?" I asked.

Hank took the paper cup from me and deposited it in a trash can we walked past. "I know his father better than him."

I blinked. Now why would that be?

CHAPTER SIX

My curiosity raced on warp speed. "What do you mean?"

Snowflakes drifted down as we walked to the Civic Center where the dance would be held tonight. I wanted to see if the fire company's auxiliary needed any help getting ready.

"Drew's father is having some boundary issues with Ivan Kline. We've been called to Mr. Ellis's house a few times to calm things down when their arguments became a little too heated.

I frowned up at Hank as we walked down the sidewalk to the center. Snow was quickly covering the ground. "What do you mean by 'too heated'?"

Hank lowered his voice. "There were threats thrown about from both gentlemen. This past summer, Mr. Ellis told Ivan to keep his grass clippings on his side of the chain link fence separating the two properties. To which Ivan replied he couldn't control where his lawn mower spit out the grass."

I shook my head. "Oh, my gosh. People behave so silly. Even though your aunt might blare her police scanner so most of the neighborhood can hear it, I'm lucky to have her living next to me."

"Yeah, I guess the topper was when Ivan found chicken bones tossed over his side of the fence." Hank leaned over and brushed snowflakes off the shoulders of my poofy coat.

"What do you do in a situation like this? What's the penalty for wayward grass clippings and chicken bones?" How foolish these men are, I thought.

"The officers who responded tried to diffuse the situation and issued the men a warning, but until they break the law, there's nothing we can do. The problem is the valuable man hours they tie up with their nonsense."

"Who is this Ivan Kline, anyway?" I asked.

A scowl marred Hank's handsome face. Oh, dear, I wasn't going to like his answer. "He's the fire chief in Summer's End."

Summer's End was a small town a few miles north of Wings Falls. Like most towns dotting the shoreline of Lake George, tourism was its main source of income. "You don't seem too happy about that. How come?" I asked.

Hank shoved his gloved hands in the pocket of his coat. "I hate to repeat gossip, but I understand he's not the most pleasant person to work under. Like the police, firemen are a brotherhood. Your coworker might be the person who saves your life. Ivan, well, he's pretty much out for himself."

"How did he ever get to be fire chief?" I asked.

"Small-town politics. His father was the fire chief before him and, before that, his grandfather. Unfortunately, he's not the stalwart person his father and grandfather were."

I nodded in understanding. "I see. Wings Falls certainly is lucky to have Jim Turner as their fire chief." Then I remembered Jane Burrows' statement. "Have you heard anything about Jim leaving the fire company?"

Hank shook his head, dislodging snowflakes that had settled amongst his wavy hair. "No, can't say I have. I hope you're wrong. He's a great fellow to work with."

The fire company and the police department often worked hand-in-hand, so I knew this was important to Hank.

I stopped in front of one of the many novelty stores lining Lake George's main street. The large window displayed T-shirts, pennants, and ball caps, all with the words Lake George printed on them or an outline of the lake. Admittedly, I had my share of these T-shirts and hats, too.

I pointed to a Lake George sweatshirt. "Do you have one of those sweatshirts?"

Hank shook his head. "Nope."

"What?" I asked in mock horror. "You've lived here more than a year and you haven't bought one, yet? Where is your upstate pride? We have to correct that situation right now." I grabbed his hand and dragged him into the store.

Hank laughed and followed me inside, not that he had any opportunity to object.

* * *

Ten minutes later, we exited the store with Hank clutching a bag containing a baby blue sweatshirt with Lake George printed on the front and the outline of the lake on the back.

I pointed to the bag. "Now you are officially an Adirondacker."

"That's a load off my mind," Hank said as we continued towards the Civic Center.

I laughed and squeezed his arm. This man I love warmed my heart with his great sense of humor.

We arrived at the center, and Hank opened the door for me. People bustled around hanging decorations. Shamrocks were taped to almost every surface. They hung from walls and doors and were even attached by strings to the ceiling. Green streamers were taped to the walls, too.

I pointed to a green-haired woman standing on a ladder at the far side of the room leaning over to tape a shamrock to a window. "Should your aunt be doing that?"

Hank shoved his bag at me and raced across the room. I hurried after him. "Aunt Gladys, what are you doing? Get down from there. You could fall. I'll hang the blasted shamrock for you."

Gladys looked down at Hank, a surprised look on her face. "If anything would cause me to fall, it would be you scaring the bejesus out of me with all of your shouting."

I glanced about the room, crowded with people setting up for tonight's dance. "We stopped in to see if you need any help, but it looks like things are pretty much under control. Where's Frank? Isn't he helping?" Although, I didn't know if a man his age should be hanging shamrocks on a tall window, either.

Gladys held on to Hank's outstretched hand as he helped her climb down from the ladder. "He's on a doughnut run."

Hank took Gladys's place on the ladder and taped the decoration to the window. He glanced down at us and asked, "Do you have anything else to hang?"

Gladys shook her head in reply. The large green bow she'd attached to her green curls swayed back and forth. "No, that about does it for me. Oh, there's Frank right now. Join us for a cup of coffee and a doughnut."

Frank strolled across the Civic Center floor towards us. His arms were ladened with boxes from Donut Haven, the town's maker of fabulous donuts.

I glanced at my Timex watch. We still had a little time before the skillet toss began. My stomach rumbled, sounding the final answer.

Hank laughed. "Is that a 'yes' for a donut?"

I nodded. "Yes, I guess it is, but we'll have to make it quick. The skillet toss begins in twenty minutes."

A grin spread across Hank's face. "You're entered into the contest?"

I slid my arm out of my coat and flexed a muscle at him. "You bet. I came in third last year, but the person to beat is Candie. She won the toss. She was a star pitcher on her softball team in school."

Hank took a step back and put his hands up in front of him. "Woah, I'd better watch myself around you two. I don't want to make you mad when you're holding a frying pan."

I laughed. "You don't have to worry. You know how limited my culinary skills are. Candie isn't far behind me with hers, either."

He reached over and tucked a curl behind my ear. Leaning close, he whispered, "Your culinary skills aren't what I love about you."

"Come on, you love birds. Let's get over to the refreshment area and have one of those donuts Frank brought us, with a cup of coffee." Gladys turned and walked towards Frank, who was headed to the kitchen area of the Civic Center with his load of goodies.

As we walked over to the counter where Frank and Gladys headed, I noticed Martha Callaway, the president of the fire company's women's auxiliary, arguing with a gentleman. I looked up at Hank and saw him frowning. "Who's Martha having words with? He looks familiar, but I can't say I know him personally."

"That's Ivan Kline. The fire chief of Summer's End."

CHAPTER SEVEN

"Why would he be arguing with Martha? She's such a sweet person. It breaks my heart thinking all she has to deal with. You do know her son is undergoing treatment for cancer?"

Hank nodded. "Yeah, we took up a collection for him at the station last week. I understand that her insurance will only cover his medical expenses, but they have to travel to Boston for his treatments, and the costs of hotels and gas are piling up for her."

Ivan Kline seemed to notice us approaching the refreshment area and backed away from Martha.

"Afternoon, Ivan. I'm surprised to see you here. The dance isn't until tonight," Hank said.

Ivan straightened to, what would be my guess, his five-foot-eight-inch height. Hank, at six-foot, still had him by a few inches. He shoved his hands in his coat pockets and threw back his shoulders, which did nothing to hide his considerable stomach. "Ummm. I thought I'd see if I could lend a hand, but it seems your group has everything under control. I'll head back up north and see you all tonight."

I turned to Martha, who looked visibly shaken by her encounter with Ivan. I placed a hand on hers. "Is everything all right?"

Martha's blonde ponytail swayed back and forth. "I'm fine. It was nothing. A little disagreement is all. Oh, I see Frank brought the donuts. Thank you, Frank. How about a cup of coffee, everyone?"

Martha dismissed what, to me, looked like a very serious and upsetting conversation with Ivan only moments before.

Frank placed the boxes of donuts on a long table set up with coffee urns at the far end. Gladys reached over and opened up the boxes. She snagged a chocolate-frosted goodie for herself then headed for the coffee.

"Here, let me help you. Regular or decaf?" Martha asked, walking towards the urns.

Gladys flicked her gnarled fingers towards the coffee urns. "Regular. None of that sissy stuff."

I did an inward groan. Since my blood pressure started north, my doctor relegated me to a lifetime of decaf.

Martha picked up a paper cup and flipped down the lever on the urn for Gladys's coffee. She pointed to the powdered creamer and sugar packets that sat next to the coffee. "Help yourself."

I stood next to Gladys. Martha looked up at me. "I'll have a decaf, please."

She gave me a weak smile. Her hand shook as she handed me my cup of coffee.

"Are you sure everything is fine? How's Jaxson doing with his treatments?"

Tears pooled in her eyes. "He's responding really well." She turned to Hank, who was standing next to me gripping a glazed donut on a napkin in his hand. "Please thank the fellows at the station for the generous donation they gave me. It's helped a lot to cover some of the expenses." She looked back at me. "I've had to take a leave of absence from my teaching position to drive Jaxson back and forth to Boston. Since I'm a single mom, all of this falls on me."

I reached across the table and hugged Martha. "If I can do anything, please let me know."

She swiped at her tears and nodded. "Thank you, I will." Turning to Frank she asked, "Now what can I get for you, young man?"

He preened at her referring to him as a "young man."

Gladys poked him in the ribs. "She's only being nice, you old coot."

I laughed. Leave it to Gladys to put things into perspective. "Come on. Let's finish up then head over to the skillet toss. Before we go, can we get you anything?"

"I hate to ask since I know you are going over to the skillet toss, but could you bring up a case of water from downstairs? The volunteers have pretty much wiped me out."

Hank tossed his crumpled napkin in the trash can situated at the end of the table. "Sure. I'll be back in a couple of minutes. Sam, do you want to wait here or come with me?"

"I'll come with." I turned to Gladys. "I'll meet you over at the skillet toss competition."

Chocolate rimmed her upper lip. "I'll be there and show you young ones how it's done."

I almost choked on the sip of coffee I had taken. "Okay, we'll join you over there in just a bit. We'll see who's the winner."

I followed Hank down the stairs to the basement area of the Civic Center. In a corner, I spotted a stack of water bottles. "Over there," I said, pointing them out to Hank.

We walked over, and Hank reached up to pull a case down, but along with it came a half dozen loose bottles lying on top. "Wow," I shouted as they tumbled down and landed at my feet.

"You all right?" Hank asked, looking me up and down for any injuries.

"Fine," I said, picking up the loose bottles and lining them up against the wall. "Let's get that case to Martha then head on over to the skillet toss."

* * *

"Watch out! Watch out!" I screamed. Candie, Gladys, our respective significant others, and I stood on a snow-covered field next to the lake. I had tossed my iron skillet just as a young girl escaped her mother's hold and ran out in front of me.

Hank raced out and snatched her into his arms. The startled child clung to his shoulders, too frightened to even cry.

Silence descended over the gathered crowd, and then the child took one look at Hank and started to bawl. The mother ran over to Hank and held her arms out for her crying daughter. The bundled-up towheaded child leaned into her mother's arms.

"Oh, Kendall, you could have been seriously hurt by the skillet if this nice man hadn't caught you. You must never leave Momma's side like that again."

With her head buried against her mother's coat, the little girl nodded and mumbled, "Yes, Momma."

The mother looked up at Hank. "Thank you for rescuing my Kendall. She turned three last week and doesn't always listen to me."

Hank smiled at the small child. "No problem, ma'am. I'm glad I could help."

The woman placed her daughter on the ground. She held on to her hand and asked, "Do you want to go to the candy shop and have Momma buy you a piece of fudge?"

Her daughter's eyes rounded at the mention of the sugary treat. "Yes, Momma."

The woman turned to Hank. "Thank you again for rescuing her." Then she led her daughter towards the promised treat.

I stumbled over to Hank, stood on my tiptoes, and placed a kiss on his stubbled cheek.

He looked down at me with a quizzical look in his eyes. "And that is for…?"

"Being the strong brave man you are. If my skillet had hit the girl, it could have caused her serious injury. Something I would not have been able to live with." A shiver ran through me at the thought of what could have happened.

Hank wrapped his arm around me. "As Inspector Gadget said, 'All in a day's work, ma'am. Any cop would have done the same.'"

I laughed and gave his arm a playful punch.

"Honey, it was such a brave thing for you to do."

I turned to see Candie and Mark standing behind me.

Mark reached out to shake Hank's hand. "I agree with my beautiful wife. Brave thing, buddy."

Red crept up Hank's face. To him, rescuing a small child was, as he had said, "all in a day's work." I was so very proud of him.

"Folks, are you ready to resume the skillet toss? Hopefully, this time without any excitement," Jim Turner asked the gathered crowd.

Shouts of *Yes* answered him.

Jim glanced down at the clipboard he held in his right hand. "Okay, next we have Candie Parker-Hogan. Candie, will you please come up to the throwing line?"

Candie leaned over and kissed Mark. "That's to give me good luck, sweetie." She sashayed up to the neon orange line sprayed on the snow. After a mighty windup, she let her skillet fly. It landed a good foot past mine.

My shoulders slumped. "I guess I'm not the winner this year."

Hank placed an arm around my shoulder and pulled me close. "There's always next year."

With a pout on my face, I said, "Yeah, I guess so."

Hank squeezed my shoulder and chuckled.

Jim ran his finger down the clipboard "Next up, Gladys O'Malley."

I pulled away from Hank to have a good view of Gladys's effort. She turned to Frank and stripped off her mittens, handing them to him. "I need to have a good grip on the skillet handle."

With shoulders thrust back and her chin jutting out, she marched up to the throwing line and accepted a skillet from a young fireman assisting Jim. She grasped the skillet handle in her bare hands and spun around as if she was about to throw a discus. With a mighty throw, she let go of the skillet. It flew across the snow-covered field and landed five feet past the marker that denoted where Candie's skillet had landed.

With a whoop and a holler, she ran over to Frank and jumped up and circled her legs around his waist.

My eyes about bugged out of my head as I watched her smother Frank's face in kisses. I thought her throw was a feat to behold for a woman her age, but her athletic ability to jump as high as she did and encircle Frank's waist with her legs left me wondering what other athletic skills she had. I shook my head. Nope, I didn't want my imagination to go there.

Candie stuck out her Passion Pink–covered lower lip. "There goes my first place."

"Don't be a sore loser," I chided her. "Any woman who can throw a skillet like she did and not wrench her back out deserves to win."

"I guess you're right."

"You know I am. Now let's go over and join the other people congratulating her." I glanced at my watch—four o'clock. The day had flown by, and there was still the Fireman's Ball to look forward to this evening. "It's getting late, and I want to go to the 5:15 Mass at Saint Anthony's so I won't have to miss the outhouse race tomorrow morning."

"Hi, Detective. This little fireman's fair is really darling, isn't it?"

CHAPTER EIGHT

———

I gave Hank a quizzical look. Who was this woman who had sidled up to Hank and placed a slender hand on his arm? I nudged Hank, hoping he got the hint to introduce me.

Little Miss Sweet Cheeks, as I named her in my mind—yes, I was being catty, but she was being a little too friendly with *my* man—seized the opportunity from Hank.

"You must be the detective's little woman. I'm Sunny, Sunny Foxx. That's Foxx with two x's." Sunny grinned up at Hank. "I'm new at the station and just getting to know all the fellows really well."

I noticed she left out the women who worked at the police station. I also noticed how well-endowed she was. If she pressed herself any closer to Hank, I was going to have to flatten her with the skillet I had tossed. I took in her long blonde hair, bleached I assumed, and her trim figure. If I was being honest, she was pretty—for an older woman, that is. I placed her age to be in her midthirties. Okay, so she was at least twenty years younger than me.

Hank, so far, hadn't said a word, but I noticed red crawling up his neck. Why was he so uncomfortable with Sunny Foxx, Ms. Foxx with two x's?

I glanced over to Candie. She gave Sunny one of her "if looks could kill" glares. "Sam, didn't you say we should be heading out so we can make the 5:15 Mass at Saint Anthony's? There's a bunch of souls I think could use our prayers." She shot a pointed look at the woman Hank tried to edge away from.

"You're right. Come on, Hank. I need to get home, but I want to stop on the way and visit with Porkchop and give him some lovin'."

If I wasn't mistaken, I swear he let out a sigh of relief when we left Sunny-girl standing by herself, but not for long. I looked back over my shoulder and saw she had edged up to Ivan Kline, who was talking to Jim Turner. From the look on Jim's face, it was more of an argument than a polite conversation between the two fire chiefs.

"Hank, you said you hadn't heard anything about Jim leaving the Wings Falls Fire Company, but is there something going on between him and Ivan Kline?"

He looked down at me with a puzzled expression. "Why do you ask? I haven't heard of any disputes between the two."

I flicked a gloved thumb over my shoulder. "Jim and Ivan look to be at odds with each other."

Hank turned to see what I was talking about. "Jim has walked away, and Sunny appears to have all of Ivan's attention right now."

I glanced in their direction. "Yes, she does. By the way… Who is she, and how do you know her?" I didn't want it to appear as if the little green monster had raised its head. I trusted Hank, but I couldn't help myself. Sunny was a little too familiar with him.

Hank let out a groan. "She's the station commander's niece and his new secretary. I don't want to make waves since I'm fairly new at the station."

"She works at the station? You're around her every day?" I screeched. Boy, did I sound like a harpy.

Hank stopped in midstride. He turned me to face him. He put a finger under my chin and raised my face so his crystal-blue eyes were looking right into mine. "You never, and I mean *never*, have to worry about how I feel about you. I love you with all my heart. I'm sorry I didn't send Sunny on her way back there, but I don't usually have women throwing themselves at me. I guess I was a bit flustered on how to handle her. It won't happen again."

I pushed back the stubborn curl of brown hair from his forehead. "I'm sorry, too, for acting like such a shrew. I know you love me, but I'm a little possessive where you are concerned. I didn't like the way she was coming on to you and, I guess, a little jealous."

A smile spread across his handsome face. "Jealous, huh?"

I glanced away as heat crawled up my neck. "Yeah, but only a wee bit." I didn't want him to get too big a head from my confession.

He laughed and grabbed my hand. "Come on, let's visit the pups, and then I'll deliver you home so you can get ready for church. I'll pick you up at seven for the dance."

I nodded then said. "Okay. I'll race you to your Jeep."

Hank laughed, and we both took off for the Civic Center parking lot.

* * *

"You look gorgeous in that gown, but then, you look gorgeous in anything you wear."

Hank's compliment warmed me as he handed my wool coat over to Drew Ellis, the young fireman who was in charge of the four-wheeler contest earlier today. Tonight, he was the coatroom attendant. I stepped out of the way so the couple in back of us could do the same. "That young man is everywhere this weekend." But the thought of seeing him smoking earlier today saddened me. He was too young to endanger his health that way.

"Yeah, thank heavens for the young members of the company. They have a lot of energy," Hank said and glanced down at me. "Why the sad face?"

I related to him about seeing Drew smoking earlier.

"Yeah, unfortunately, the long stretches of time between incidents leads to boredom, and a number of guys fill those long hours with smoking." He took my elbow and guided me through the crowd.

I reached for Hank's hand as we walked into the event space of the Civic Center. The room looked fabulous. It had a real festive air to it, with all the Saint Patrick's Day decorations.

Couples stood together talking and laughing with friends. I spotted mugs of green beer in many hands.

"You polished up fairly good yourself, tonight," I said in return for him complimenting my dress. I ran the fingers of my free hand over the lapels of his sports coat. I had donned an emerald-green dress that clung to all the right places on my body.

"Over here, Sam, Hank. Over here."

I turned in the direction of the voice calling to us and smiled when I saw my cousin and Mark standing by the buffet line. Candie had her arm entwined with Mark's. I grinned at the leprechauns dancing across his tie. His sports coat was a dark green tweed he'd paired with a lighter shade of green wool pants. Candie's pale green knit dress was a perfect complement to her auburn curls, caught up in a loose bun at the nape of her neck. Loose tendrils framed her face.

"Here, grab a plate, and let's hit the buffet line before it gets picked over."

I laughed as Candie shoved a plate at me. True, it was later in the evening then I was used to eating, but I'd been too busy making myself "gorgeous" for Hank to eat anything after arriving home after Mass. I scanned the buffet table. Three of my favorite Wings Falls restaurants were serving up food tonight. Brian and Susan Mayfield's Momma Mia's offered a number of delicious Italian-themed dishes, Clint Higgins, owner of The Smiling Pig, had warming pans filled with his mouth-watering barbeque. His sister, Marybeth, was a fellow Loopy Lady. At the end of the line stood Hank's brother, Aaron, along with his girlfriend, Joy, and the owner of Sweetie Pie's Café, Franny Goodway. Tonight, Franny had brought along a variety of Southern desserts she and her restaurant were famous for. I needed to rein in my sweet tooth, or I would have skipped by all the other yummy offerings and headed right to the dessert part of the dinner. A slice of Franny's banana cream pie definitely had my name on it.

"Hi, Susan," I said as I approached her section of the buffet table. "What are you and Brian serving tonight? It all smells so delicious."

With a plastic-gloved hand, Susan pointed to the warming pans in front of her. "Here we have spaghetti and meatballs." She lifted the lid off the next warming dish. "Brian also prepared his famous lasagna for tonight, too."

I turned to Hank. "Why don't you take the spaghetti and meatballs, and I'll share my lasagna with you? That way we can indulge in both and not become overstuffed."

He nodded. "Sounds like a plan."

Candie waggled her jewel-ladened fingers at me. "Oh. Sam, I like your idea." She turned to Mark, who was behind her in line. "Sweetie, why don't we do the same?"

"Honey, whatever you'd like," Mark said.

I smiled. I doubted there would ever be a day when he didn't think what she said was positively brilliant.

After Susan filled my plate with lasagna, I scooted farther down the line to Clint Higgins's food. Marybeth, who usually worked nights at the Wings Falls Hospital as a nurse, held court over the chafing dishes filled with food from The Smiling Pig's menu.

"Helping Clint out tonight?" I motioned toward his chafing dishes. "What has he brought?"

Marybeth lifted the stainless-steel lid off of a warming dish. "Here we have honey barbeque wings." She leaned over the table and whispered to me. "Personally, they are my favorite."

I laughed. "Me, too. Hank and I are sharing tonight so we can sample some of everything. I'll take the wings, and he can fill his plate up with whatever you have in the next dish."

"Barbeque sliders." Marybeth lifted the next lid off. The mouth-watering aroma of pulled pork wafted towards me. My taste buds did a happy dance. "Give me a serving of the wings and place two of those sliders on Hank's plate."

Hank leaned over my shoulder. "From the smell of those sliders, you'd better add a couple more to my plate. I don't think I'll be satisfied with just one."

Marybeth laughed and followed Hank's request.

Mark edged forward. "Hey, buddy. Leave some for Candie and me."

"We've got plenty more warming up in the kitchen," Marybeth said.

"That's a good thing," Candie said. "I haven't eaten since the donuts Frank brought this afternoon. I'm about to perish from hunger."

Next down the table were the desserts Franny had brought from her café. My mouth watered, eyeing the delicious-looking confections. I definitely had my hopes on a slice of the banana cream pie. "Hi, Aaron. Did you bake this?" I asked, pointing to the pie covered with a mound of whipped cream. Aaron was Hank's baby brother. He moved north from Albany last year. Aaron had been hanging with a pretty rough crowd, and his mother hoped living with Hank would be a good influence on him. Not only had he given up his wild behavior, but he was working at Sweetie Pie's and going to the local community college to improve his culinary skills.

Aaron puffed up his chest. "Yep. It's Franny's recipe, but I put my special touch on it."

I licked my lips. "After I finish this," I said, holding out my plate to him, "I'll be back for a slice of it. Make sure you save me one."

"Will do," Aaron said. Joy placed her arm through his and smiled at us. Her dark skin was a contrast to the white apron she'd slipped over her head. I was very proud of what Aaron was doing with his life and equally happy that he'd found such a wonderful girlfriend in Joy.

"Oh, Ivan. You say the funniest things."

I turned to spot the owner of the voice that carried down the food line. Sunny Foxx, with two x's. She wore a skintight black dress and giggled up at Ivan Kline. I did a mental sigh of relief. At least she'd switched her attention away from Hank.

Candie leaned over and whispered in my ear, "Memaw Parker would say that woman's dress is so short you could see her religion."

I laughed. "She'd certainly be right. I hope it doesn't cause her any problems."

CHAPTER NINE

————

I spotted four empty seats at a round table. I leaned over to ask the back of a woman's head, "Mind if we join you?"

When she turned, my eyes widened in surprise. This had to be the first time I'd seen Jane Burrows in something other than the khakis and sweater sets she usually wore. She looked very attractive in a navy knit dress.

Jim Turner was dressed in his fire chief's uniform. He swallowed then pointed with his fork at the empty seats. "Please do."

Hank pulled out my seat while Mark pulled out a chair for Candie. I glanced down at the food piled on Hank's and my plates. "I wonder if we were eating with our eyes at the food line?"

Candie looked at Mark's and her plates. "I was thinking the same thing."

"I'm certainly going to give it my best try to polish it off," Hank said, sitting down.

With a fork poised over his plate, Mark said, "Me, too."

"Turner, going to have any fireworks tonight?" a slurred voice asked in back of us.

Jim clenched his jaw and looked up at the source of the comment, Ivan Kline. "Ivan, you know I'm not a fan of fireworks."

"Yeah, I guess you're not. They could cause a lot of harm if not handled correctly. Right, Chief? Thanks to you, my brother learned it the hard way," Ivan said, a smirk crossing his face.

Jim ignored Ivan and focused on the plate of food in front of him.

Sunny stood next to him, clinging to his arm. A glass wobbled in her fingers. "Ivan, I need a refill. Will you get me another glass of wine?"

Ivan held up his empty beer glass. "Sure. It looks like I could use a refill, too." He turned, and the two of them weaved their way back to the bar, bumping into people on their way.

"What was that all about?" I asked. "They both look like they've had enough to drink."

Jim stared at his plate as if it held the answer to some deep mystery. "I couldn't tell you, and frankly, I don't care, either."

Candie turned towards me and mouthed, *Whoa...?*

I shrugged in return. I had no idea what the issue between Jim and Ivan was, but it seemed like they had some history between them. And why did Ivan mention his brother? I looked up at Hank, but he shook his head as if he didn't have an answer either.

Raised voices caught my attention. I turned to see Sunny Foxx shaking a finger at a scruffy-looking fellow who appeared to be about her age. He ran a hand through his long blond hair. His clothes were disheveled, borderline dirty. He certainly didn't appear to be one of the guests at the dance, who were all dressed in their finest.

Hank started to rise from his seat but then sat back down as Ivan approached the fellow and spoke to him. Whatever he said caused the younger man to leave.

*   *   *

I smiled at the group sitting at my table. "I love your idea, Jane, about Porkchop wearing a fireman's helmet and gear. Could be a whole new calendar focus for him." I leaned back in my chair and groaned. The evening had been filled with great conversation and a fabulous meal.

A thumping sound came through the PA system. Hank looked towards the stage at the far end of the room. "It looks like the DJ is about to start. Care to dance?" he asked, rising from his chair and holding out a hand to me.

I nodded. "That will be one way to work off all the food I've eaten. I really should have said no to the banana cream pie, but it looked too delicious to pass up."

Jane placed her napkin next to her plate and started to rise. "You folks enjoy yourself. Jim's going to run me home. Mother had a bit of a headache before I left the house tonight, and I want to check on her."

"Okay. I hope your mom is feeling better. See you later, Jim." I waved at him. He took Jane's arm as she stood.

"Oh, I'll be back as soon as I drop off Jane. I need to be here since my fire company is sponsoring tonight," he said as he placed a hand on Jane's elbow.

Candie stood and tugged on Mark's hand. "Come on, Mark. Let's join Sam and Hank on the dance floor."

* * *

I pointed to the Loopy Ladies' outhouse as it sat with the other contestants. "I see the guys attached the skis to the bottom."

"I'm ready to take my throne and show everyone that the Loopy Ladies reign supreme."

I laughed. Gladys had propped a gold paper crown on top of her green curls.

We, meaning all twelve of us Loopy Ladies, were gathered on the snowy field next to the Civic Center, ready for the race to begin. Missing were the men who were going to push the outhouse and Gladys to the finish line. Hank mentioned they had some business to attend to and would join us here.

"I hope they arrive sooner rather than later. I'm freezing." I clasped my mittened hands together to try to keep their circulation going. I reached down and straightened the fleece-lined sweater I had slipped onto Porkchop before I left the house. He shook his front paw. I'd also added booties to his outfit to keep his paws warm. Hank's Nina stood next to him also sporting a sweater and booties. I was minding her while Hank went to join the men.

Candie tucked a blanket around her babies. They lay sleeping in the pet carriage she rocked back and forth much like a momma would to calm her child. "I think I see them coming now." She pointed to a group of four men crossing the snow-covered field.

I blinked then blinked again. What was approaching us were three men dressed as court pages. Mark, Hank, and Brian wore floppy hats with a feather sticking out of the brim, a tight-fitting jacket that ended at the waist, and what my Memaw would call puffy bloomers that came to their knees. Tights encased their muscled legs. To complete their outfits, on their feet were shoes that curled up at the toes. The men surrounded Frank. He wore a purple regal robe and carried a gold-colored royal staff in the crook of his right arm. Like Gladys, a gold crown topped his thinning gray hair.

"All hail His Majesty, Frank, also known as Pookie Bear, is here to pay homage to his queen, Gladys, and soon-to-be winner of the Wings Falls Firemen's outhouse race." Hank, Mark, and Brian halted before Gladys and performed a most elegant bow.

Tears of laughter streamed down the Loopy Ladies' faces. Gladys preened at the attention, enjoying it to its fullest extent. She tottered through the snow towards Frank, trying not to trip. Even though the snow in the race area had been tamped down, there were still ruts that could turn the ankle of an unsuspecting person.

Hank pointed towards the outhouse. "Come on. It's time to get the outhouse—or should I say Her Majesty's throne—in place for the race."

"Yes, we have to remove the blanket you nailed to the front and make sure all the rugs haven't shifted in the move from my garage to here," I said, walking over to the tent that held the outhouses.

As we approached the area, I noticed a number of empty plastic water bottles scattered about the ground. I frowned. Usually, people in the area were very careful to dispose of their trash. Even the tourists wanted to keep the Adirondacks clean and forever wild.

"Do you believe this?" I asked, pointing to the bottles.

Candie, pushing her pet carriage before her, shook her head. "People can be so disrespectful."

Porkchop pulled on his leash and started to whine as we approached the outhouse. He let out a fierce growl then tore out of my hand. His leash bounced on the ground as he raced towards the outhouse.

I ran after him. "Porkchop!" My pup was on a mission and ignored my shouts.

He nosed his long body under the blanket nailed to the front of the outhouse. A moment later, he reappeared with a glove in his mouth. He scurried over and dropped it at my feet.

I bent and picked it up and frowned. I didn't recognize the glove and didn't remember there being one in the outhouse when the guys loaded it onto Brian's truck Saturday. Maybe one of them had forgotten theirs when they delivered the outhouse here.

I turned to Hank, who had Nina nestled in his arms. Being a miniature bulldog, and on the small side, she fit easily into the crook of his arm. If I thought Porkchop was spoiled, Hank's bulldog had Porkchop beat by a mile. "Did one of you guys forget a glove last night?"

Hank shook his head. The feather on his regal cap swayed back and forth. "No. We tacked the blanket down pretty good. But look, one edge. It's flapping. It was secure when we left it."

Hank placed Nina on the ground and handed me her leash. He hurried over to the outhouse and pulled back the blanket. I, the Loopy Ladies, and Gladys's court gasped. Before us on the throne sat a frozen Ivan Kline.

CHAPTER TEN

Hank motioned for me to join him. "I don't have my phone on me. Do you have yours with you?"

I tried to avoid looking at Ivan's frozen face, but unfortunately, there was a bit of humor in this deadly situation. "Yeah, I guess there was no place to put it in your tights." I dug into my coat pocket, pulled out my phone, and handed it to him.

I backed away from the outhouse as he placed Nina at his feet. He punched the number of the local police department into the phone.

Helen Garber, dressed in a neon-green wool coat, stepped towards me. She pointed at the outhouse. "What's happened in there? Ivan doesn't look very good. Will he be all right?"

The pompom on my knit hat bounced against my head as I shook my head. "I believe he might be dead."

Helen placed gloved hands on her ample hips. "*Humph.* Doesn't surprise me. He was a nasty person."

My eyes widened at her answer. What did Helen know about Ivan Kline? Did she have issues with him?

Hank ended his call. "Ladies, you'd better go into the Civic Center. An ambulance, and I'm sure the police, will be here soon. They will probably want to talk to all of us."

Brian Mayfield, one of Gladys's court attendees, took charge of herding the Loopy Ladies towards the center.

Gladys walked past me with her head on Frank's shoulder. His arm encircled her. "My reign as queen has been cut short," she moaned. Her crown, which sat so regally nestled in her green curls moments before, had slipped down her forehead.

"Love bug, you'll always be the queen of my heart." Frank wrapped his royal robe around her.

I decided to remain with Hank. Candie and Mark also stood next to us. A squad car marked with the Lake George police logo skidded to a stop on the road next to the park. The driver's door swung open, and a police officer stepped out. He adjusted his gun belt then walked towards us. "Morning, Detective, Mayor. What do we have here?" His eyes widened as he looked into the outhouse. "What the… Is that Ivan Kline? He doesn't look in too good a shape."

Hank stepped aside so the officer could get closer to the outhouse. "Fred, I'd say that's an understatement. It looks like he froze to death out here." Hank nodded towards the outhouse then turned to me. "Sam, this is Chief Fred Kelly, head of the Lake George PD."

Fred tipped his uniform hat at me. "Glad to meet you, ma'am."

I smiled in return to his greeting. "Same here, Fred."

Mark stepped up. "What brings you out of the station, Fred? Usually, your men respond to a call."

Fred hooked his thumbs in his gun belt. "The flu has played havoc with my guys. I barely have enough men to cover a shift."

I looked up at Hank. "You haven't had that problem at your station, have you?" The local news stations had reported a flu outbreak upstate, but so far, I hadn't heard of anyone I knew coming down with it.

Hank shook his head. The feather on his hat floated about his forehead. "No, thank heavens. We've been lucky."

Candie, who had stood silent next to me, spoke up. "It's been the same at City Hall, right Mark?"

Like Hank's, the feather on Mark's hat bobbed when he nodded. "That's right, honey. So, what do you think, Fred? Can we turn investigating Ivan's death over to you since it happened in your town?"

Hank turned to Fred. "Yeah, it'd be a relief, for once not to have to be involved with a local death."

Fred took off his uniform hat and ran a hand through his wavy gray hair. "Fellows, I hate to impose, but I'm really short on manpower, and since you probably know most of the people who are involved in this Firemen's Convention, what with Wings Falls Fire Company sponsoring it, I'd really appreciate your help."

Hank nodded. "I'm certainly not going to say no. You and your men have been there for Wings Falls PD when we've needed them. I'll phone the station right now and ask for backup." Like most small towns, Lake George and Wings Falls had a Mutual Aide Agreement that allowed individual towns to help each other out when necessary. Hank punched in the station's number on my phone he still clutched in his hand.

I smiled. I couldn't have been prouder of my man. He was there for his fellow brothers in uniform no matter what, even when he was dressed as a court page.

So far, the pups had all been very patient. I held Porkchop against the warmth of my body. Dixie and Annie slept soundly snuggled under a fleece blanket in their carriage as Candie rocked it back and forth. Nina laid her body across Hank's shoes. The cold was starting to seep through all the layers of clothing I had donned this morning, but I was sure I wasn't as cold as Hank and Mark in the thin costumes they had planned to wear for only a short amount of time during the race.

As if noticing the guys' attire for the first time, Fred's bushy left eyebrow rose. "Umm, unusual choice of outfits you're wearing."

Hank and Mark both chuckled. "Yeah, and not the warmest either. It's a long story. Let's just say we were trying to make an old lady's day."

Now it was my turn for my eyebrows to skyrocket. If Gladys ever heard her nephew referring to her as an old lady, she'd erupt like an overflowing volcano. Hank had better take cover because the fallout would not be pretty.

I turned towards the sound of sirens fast approaching the park. Two black and white squad cars from Wings Falls PD skidded to a halt on the snow-covered ground. An ambulance pulled up to the curb right behind them. Out of the first squad car emerged two young officers I had met before, Officers March and Reed. New guys to the force but learning fast. I groaned and rolled my eyes towards the clear blue sky overhead when I saw who exited from the second car—my childhood nemesis, Joe Peters. He and I had a history going back to when we attended kindergarten together, and it wasn't a good one. Unfortunately, I was the one who reported he had peed in the school's sandbox, and he never forgave me. It wasn't my fault kids nicknamed him Sandy for his lack of potty manners. He'd love to blame me for a murder, any murder, and throw away the keys. He'd done it on more than one occasion.

Well, this was one death he wouldn't be able to pin on me. Last night, I'd seen Ivan downing the green beers pretty heavily. It was my guess he unfortunately drank too many, wandered outside, needed a place to rest, and picked our outhouse for that purpose. He probably tore back the blanket, sat down, passed out, and then froze to death. It was a tragedy, but not one of my making.

From the passenger side of Joe's squad car emerged Doc Cordone. He was the medical examiner for the county. I frowned, wondering why he was here. Since I'd been involved in other murders, I was acquainted with Doc. Had Hank requested for him to come? Did he suspect there was more to Ivan's death than a drunk passing out in the cold and freezing to death?

"Hi Doc," I said as the older gentleman approached the outhouse.

A wool knit cap was pulled over his thinning gray hair. His rubber boots slapped against the snow. A long wool coat hung loosely from his shoulders. He pulled a pair of rubber gloves out of his pocket. "Hi, Sam. What have you got for me this time, Hank?"

"Hi, Doc. You know Fred here." Hank flicked his hand towards Fred.

"Sure, we met on more than one occasion before he became head of Lake George's PD. I heard the flu has got your guys pretty bad."

"That's right, Doc. I've asked Hank and his men to give us a hand since we are so low staffed," Fred said.

"Okay, let me see what you've got here." Doc walked towards the outhouse. The EMTs stepped aside as he started to examine Ivan's body. Since Ivan was already dead, there wasn't much for them to do. Doc poked at Ivan's jacket, felt his hair and face, and then turned towards those of us gathered near the outhouse.

"This fellow didn't die a natural death."

CHAPTER ELEVEN

———

Hank leaned closer to Ivan's body. "You think there is foul play involved in his death?"

Doc Cordone looked over his wire-rimmed glasses and nodded. "Yep. Someone soaked the poor guy with a liquid. I'm going to presume it is water, but until we get him to the morgue and I can run tests, don't take that as the gospel truth. He's also got a pretty good lump on the back of his head. Don't go ruling out murder as his cause of death."

Candie and I looked at each other with wide eyes. Her Passion Pink–covered lips mouthed, *Murder?*

I shrugged. A chill ran through me, and this time it wasn't from the cold air whipping at my face. Who would want to kill Ivan Kline? I thought back to yesterday at the Civic Center and last night at the Firemen's Ball. A few people came to mind—Drew Ellis, Martha Callaway, Sunny Foxx. And what did Helen Garber mean by her comment earlier? Unfortunately, from the snide remark Ivan made to Jim Turner last night, I'd have to add him to the list, too. And I couldn't forget the unknown disheveled fellow who showed up at the Fireman's Ball. He certainly didn't like Sunny cozying up to Ivan. Who was he?

Could any of them have been mad enough to kill Ivan Kline and in such a cruel manner?

What would their motives be? Had the land feud between the young fireman Drew Ellis's father and Ivan come to a head? Was he defending his father's honor? Martha looked pretty upset with Ivan yesterday when we were at the Civic Center. What could that have been about? Sunny Foxx—Hank's station commander's niece… Had she bitten off more than she could handle when she cuddled up to Ivan? I knew Helen Garber had a nasty way with her tongue at times, but violence was never in her nature. Did Helen and Ivan have a history none of us knew about? We all had something in our past we'd kept hidden. Could the same be true for her? And lastly, Jim Turner. Nope, I wasn't even going to consider him. Nope, never. Not kind sweet Jim.

"Did you hear me?"

I shook myself out of my reverie and glanced at my cousin. "Did you say something to me?"

Candie stomped her feet to keep their circulation moving. "I've been flapping my lips while you were staring off into space. What's on your mind? No, better yet, let's get ourselves and the fur babies inside, out of this cold. The wind is picking up and chilling me to the bone."

"That sounds like a good idea. The guys are busy dealing with Ivan's death." Candie and I walked over to Mark and Hank, who were talking to the gathered police officers and Doc Cordone.

I tapped Hank on the shoulder. He turned towards me and smiled. "Sorry. I guess I'm a little tied up here."

A smile crossed my lips. "Yeah, I'd say you are. Candie and I are going to go inside. Do you want me to take Nina with me?"

Nina shook her body. Porkie leaned over and planted a doggie kiss on her snout. I believed he was secretly in love with her.

"That would be a great help. And here's the keys to my Jeep and your phone back. I'll get a ride home later from one of the guys here." He nodded towards the cruisers parked next to the curb then bent and placed a kiss on the top of my head.

Candie pushed the doggie stroller towards me. She said her goodbyes to Mark, too, giving him a kiss and hug. From the besotted look on his face, I couldn't imagine him ever entertaining the thought of leaving Candie. We walked towards the Civic Center, Candie with her stroller and me with Porkchop and Nina on their leashes.

"Who do ya'll think did Ivan in? He sure wasn't pleasant-looking, what with those eyes of his staring straight ahead and the tiny icicles hanging off his hair and uniform."

I blinked at my cousin's direct question. Like Helen, she didn't mince words, but she did it in a more Southern Belle, genteel manner. No, the image of Ivan would stay with me for quite a while.

Porkchop and Nina tugged on their leashes. They were just as anxious to get into the warmth of the Civic Center as I was. "I don't know for sure, but I have a few thoughts about potential suspects."

Candie pulled her pet stroller to a halt. I was so engrossed in my thoughts about the suspects, I had walked a few feet ahead of her before I realized she wasn't beside me.

"What? Come on. Let's get of this cold." I turned back to see her staring wide-eyed at me.

"Sugar, you can't leave me hanging like that." She waggled her fingers at me, the sun reflecting off the baubles on her fingers. "Who murdered Ivan?"

I shrugged. "I'm only guessing from things I observed yesterday, but it's too cold to talk about it out here."

We continued the short distance to the Civic Center. I pulled open the heavy glass front door. The sound of chattering people hit my ears. A growl rumbled up Porkchop's throat. "Is all this excitement a bit much for you, Porkie?" I leaned down and stroked the raised fur on his back. Nina edged closer to my legs.

I glanced around the room. The shamrocks that were so carefully taped to the walls yesterday now hung drunkenly, many upside down. The floor was littered with discarded paper napkins and plates from last night's buffet. Folding chairs, once surrounding the tables where we dined, were stacked on rolling carts to be stored away for future use. The cleaning crew was busy sweeping and arranging the center for an upcoming function.

Candie pointed to the far corner of the room. The Loopy Ladies plus Frank sat at two round tables, their heads together. Brian sat next to his wife, Susan. "I bet they're talking about what happened outside with Ivan."

"I'd say you'd be correct."

"Hi, ladies, Frank, and Brian," Candie said as we approached the tables.

Greetings of *hi* and *hello* came in return.

Frank sat with his arm across Gladys's shoulder. While tears no longer streaked down her wrinkled cheeks, her crown still perched crookedly on her green curls. A forlorn look rested on her face. "So, what's going on outside there?" Gladys asked, her eyes bloodshot from crying.

Porkchop and Nina curled up at my feet as I took a seat across from Gladys. Candie parked her pet stroller next to her chair. Annie and Dixie poked their heads up, glanced around at the group, and then yawned and snuggled back under their fleece blanket.

"The EMTs and police have arrived on the scene. It's pretty busy out there. Doc Cordone arrived, too, with Sergeant Peters," I said, as I dug into my Fendie purse for a treat for Nina and Porkchop.

Patsy Ikeda's eyebrows rose. Like me, she often brought her dog, Hana, a beautiful Japanese Spitz, to The Ewe on Monday mornings when we gathered for our weekly hooking sessions. "Why would someone from the Wings Falls PD come, and why Doc Cordone?"

How much of what I saw and heard outside should I divulge to the group? True, like Wings Falls, Lake George was a small town and not much stayed secret for a long time, but I didn't think Hank would be very happy with me if I was the source of the local gossip. "All I know is Chief Kelly mentioned to Hank that his department was low on staff because of an outbreak of flu amongst his guys. He asked if the Wings Falls PD could help with the investigation. Hank, of course, said yes. And Doc Cordone only wants to make sure Ivan died of natural causes."

Candie poked me in the ribs. We both knew that wasn't true. A murderer was out there, somewhere.

CHAPTER TWELVE

———

I shot Candie a side-eyed glare. If she wanted to spill the beans about Ivan's death, let her, but I didn't want Hank to find out I was the blabbermouth.

Helen patted her flaming red hair she wore fashioned in a French twist then glanced at her watch. "If that toad, Ivan, died a natural death, why are we still hanging out here? I need to leave. I told Orville I'd be home in time to watch the Jets game with him." Orville was her husband. A slim fellow who had taught math at the Wings Falls High School. Now his passion was the New York Jets football team. Helen once mentioned he always wore his Jets sweatshirt and baseball cap when watching his favorite football team. I wondered if Helen did the same.

This was the second time Helen spoke disparagingly of Ivan Kline. What had gone on between the two of them for her to have such ill feelings towards him?

Murmurs for the reason we were still here at the center circled the group. "All I know is the police might have a few questions for us because he died in our outhouse and we were all present when his body was discovered."

Helen flopped back in her chair and folded her arms across her ample chest. A scowl rested on her full face. She was obviously not happy with my answer.

The door to the Civic Center swung open. Officers March and Reed strode in and walked directly to our tables. Their heavy boots echoed off the hall's tile floor as they approached us.

Officer Reed smiled at our group. He removed his hat and tucked it under his arm. "Hello, ladies, gentlemen. Thank you for being so patient and waiting for us to ask you a few questions. Officer March, here, and I will try to get this over quickly so you can be on your way."

Officer March nodded to the group. His hat, likewise, resided under his arm.

"Oh, my, you two are cuties. If I were younger—I'm not going to say how much younger; that's my secret—you could warm my tootsies on these cold winter nights. But I've got my Frank here to do the job."

I whipped my head around. Had I really heard Gladys correctly? She was flirting with these young officers who had to be in their midtwenties.

Gladys gave me a wide-eyed innocent look then glanced around at the rest of the group. "What? I ain't dead yet. Right, Pookie Bear?"

Frank patted Gladys's hand. "Yep, Snookums, you're as randy as a spring chicken."

Laughter erupted around the table.

Candie leaned towards me. "I sure hope I have her energy when I'm her age."

"I hear you," I whispered back.

I glanced at the two officers. Poor Officer March. His face had turned a brilliant shade of red. Officer Reed fidgeted with his hat. They, obviously, weren't used to a woman their grandmother's age making a pass at them.

Officer March ran a hand over his buzzed sandy blond hair. A haircut that closely mimicked Officer Reed's tightly curled black hair. "Ummm, folks, if you don't mind, Officer Reed and I will begin asking you about last night and what you might have seen. We'll split you folks up so the questioning can go faster, and we'll have you out of here in no time."

I turned to Candie. "This shouldn't take long. Hank gave me the keys to his Jeep. When we're finished, do you want me to run you home, or would you like to have Mark pick you up at my place?"

Annie stirred in the pet stroller. Candie leaned over and tucked the blanket around Annie's small body. "I'd appreciate a ride to your place. I'll give Mark a call and tell him to pick me up there."

I raised an eyebrow. "Things still not going well between the two of you?"

Candie fussed with the blanket and wouldn't look me in the eyes. She shrugged her shoulders. "It could be better. This morning wasn't too bad."

I looked into my cousin's sad violet eyes and tried to read what was going on in her pretty head. "Mark was loving towards you this morning when we were in the park."

Candie blinked back unshed tears. "We were in public. He'd never let anyone know what was happening at home. I'm sure he knows I've shared our business with you and he's not too happy about it."

I sat up rigid in my folding chair. "Mark has to know we're Parkers and we stick together."

A smile lifted Candie's lips. "You're right. Memaw Parker drilled that into us from when we were no bigger than a June bug."

*　*　*

"That didn't take long. Officers March and Reed were really organized." I placed the key into the ignition of Hank's Jeep. Except for Dixie, who lay curled up on Candie's lap in the passenger seat, the fur babies were settled in the back seat..

"They'll make good officers, especially after dealing with the Loopy Ladies."

I had to agree. We were a conglomeration of personalities. "Yes, but it didn't appear that the ladies had much to contribute to the investigation. No one saw or heard anything. Maybe Ivan was drunk and just wandered outside. He could have gotten curious and wanted to see what was behind the blanket nailed to our outhouse."

Candie stroked the fur on Dixie's back. She turned to me and said, "Maybe so, but where did the icicles come from that had formed on his hair and jacket?"

I turned the key and the Jeep roared to life. Unlike my VW Bug, Hank's car had a more powerful engine. I had never driven it before and hoped I could manage all this horsepower. I shifted into reverse and backed out of the parking space then pointed the car towards home. I mulled over Candie's question. "Doc Cordone does suspect foul play—at least, that's what he said before we came inside the Center."

"Yes, he did, but who do you think would do such a mean ol' thing?"

I thought about the people who I'd seen yesterday who had words with Ivan and hoped it wasn't any of them. Then my mind flashed to the empty water bottles lying on the ground. Were those the ones that had been used on the now-dead man?

* * *

Traffic was light for a Sunday afternoon. That wouldn't be the situation in a couple of months when the weather warmed up and tourists flocked up north to enjoy our beautiful mountains and lakes. Fifteen minutes after driving out of the Civic Center's parking lot, I pulled Hank's Jeep into my driveway. I turned off the Jeep and looked over at Candie and smiled. Along with all the pets, she was sound asleep. Candie snored softly. A thin stream of drool ran out of the corner of her mouth and down her chin. If I ever mentioned she snored, she would vehemently deny it, saying that no properly raised Southern woman did such a thing.

I touched her arm.

"What? What?" She blinked and looked around her. She swiped at the drool on her chin. "Oh, my. I must have nodded off."

My hand swept the front and back seats. "Yes, you did, along with all our babies. Let's get inside, feed them, and then let them out back to do their business."

"Sounds good. It's been a stressful day so far, and I'm sure they're hungry. I know I'm starving."

"How about after we settle them down, we head over to Sweetie Pie's for a bite to eat? I imagine the guys will be tied up for most of the day."

Candie slid out of the car with Dixie cradled in her arm. "Oh, that sounds wonderful. I would love some barbeque right about now."

My stomach rumbled. "I think my tummy is saying a big fat yes to your suggestion. How about we call the guys and tell them our plans?"

Candie reached into the back of the Jeep for her pet stroller. "You go ahead and call Hank. I'll get in touch with Mark later."

I jerked up, hitting my head on the top of the doorframe. Were things that bad in the Hogan household?

CHAPTER THIRTEEN

———

I slipped my arms out of the sleeves of my hunter green down coat and slid it next to me on the booth's seat then placed my black Kenneth Cole shoulder bag on top of it. Designer purses were a weakness of mine. Luckily, I'd been able to score this bargain on eBay. I hadn't bought a new one in months, but I saw this beauty and had to have it. With Dixie and the pups settled by the fireplace in my house, Candie and I had headed over to Sweetie Pie's Café for a bite to eat. I drove but switched out Hank's Jeep for my beloved VW. I felt more in control of my Bug than I did driving his vehicle. I glanced around the restaurant. As usual, it was hopping on a Sunday night. Candie and I were lucky to grab our favorite booth, one that looked out onto the street so we could people watch as we ate. I spied Hank's brother, Aaron, through the opening on the far wall of the restaurant that looked into the kitchen. I waved, but he was too busy tending the grill to notice me.

"Oh, look." Candie pointed to the blackboard hanging on the wall behind the counter lined with stools. "Barbeque sandwiches are on special tonight. And my fave—sweet potato fries, too. My stomach is going to think it's back in Hainted Holler when I send all that yummy food its way."

Franny, the owner, was from the south and moved north about the same time Candie did, fifteen years ago. Wings Falls was lucky Franny brought her fabulous southern recipes with her. Her restaurant has been a success since she flipped over her open sign.

I nodded. "It sounds like a winning combination for me, too. I'll have the same."

"Ladies, care for a cup of coffee while you're deciding what to order?"

Startled, I turned towards Franny. "Oh, my! I didn't hear you approach, Franny, but yes, I'd love a cup of coffee. Decaf, you know, for me."

Franny laughed. Her long, curly black hair was pulled back in a ponytail. Like her restaurant, Franny's waitress uniform was a throwback to the 50s. She wore a pink dress that skimmed her thin body. A black apron was tied around her waist, and a lace-trimmed handkerchief flowed out of the breast pocket.

"I'll have the same, but none of that sissy stuff Sam is having. Bring on the caffeine for me."

Franny and I laughed at Candie's comment. It wasn't my fault that my blood pressure started to rise when I went through my divorce.

"I believe we already know what we want to order, too," I said, shooing away the plastic-coated menus Franny held out to us.

Franny slid an order pad from the pocket of her apron then reached up for the pen tucked over her ear. "Okay, shoot. What will y'all have?"

"Today's special," Candie and I both said at once. The three of us laughed.

Franny jotted down our requests. "I guess you two did know what you wanted. I'll be right back with your coffee."

When Franny left, I leaned over the red Formica-topped table towards the jukebox situated at the end. I flipped through the selection cards. "Who do you want to listen to? Roy Orbison or Elvis?" Like the café, the music selection was mostly from the 50s, too. Franny had thrown in a few Donnie Osmond songs, too, to satisfy my teenage crush.

Candie closed her eyes. "I believe tonight I'd like the soothing sounds of Roy."

My eyebrows shot up. She wasn't as big a fan of Roy as I was and usually opted for Elvis. "Okay, spill the beans. What's up?"

She heaved a sigh. "What? After this morning's events, can't I enjoy some mellow music to soothe my nerves?"

I leaned across the tabletop. "Yeah, and Dixie and Porkchop are BFFs."

Candie waved her fingers at me. "Okay, okay. I told you earlier that Mark and I are having a few issues. I just don't know what to do. I'm not going to give up my precious Dixie, but I don't want to lose Mark, either. I'm in a tizzy as how to make things better." Tears gathered on the lashes of her violet eyes.

I reached across the table and took one of her hands in mine. "Mark loves you. You know that. He'd never ask you to abandon

Dixie. So, let's think of a way to solve this problem. Dixie was a big fan of Mark before you had to surrender Cuddles to the shelter. Right?"

Candie gave me a weak smile. "Yes. Even though it was for only a short amount of time, we were one happy family."

"But now, if I understand things correctly, Dixie blames Mark for Cuddles not being a part of your household?"

Candie's auburn curls bounced against her shoulders as she nodded her answer to my question. "Yes, she thinks since Mark left the house with Cuddles and didn't have him when he returned, he is the reason Cuddles is no longer with us. She is right angry with him. You saw that nasty scratch she gave him when he tried to snuggle with me on the sofa the other night."

I rested my chin on my hand. "Hmm. what can we do to convince Dixie that Mark isn't the bad guy and to make everything perfect in the Parker-Hogan household again?" My eyes widened. "I've got it." I leaned over and whispered my brilliant idea to Candie.

She sat up in the red vinyl-covered booth seat and clapped her hands. A smile spread across her face. "I believe it will work." She bounced in her seat with happiness.

"I hate to break up what looks like a happy moment, but here's your order." Franny balanced a large tray, filled with their order, on her shoulder.

Candie and I both scooched back in our seats to give Franny room to place our plates ladened with barbeque sandwiches and sweet potato fries on the table in front of us.

Candie eyed the plate Franny set before her. "Franny, I'm so hungry, I thought my stomach was fixin' to disown me. This barbeque will sure make it happy."

Sweetie Pie's buzzed with excitement. Snippets of conversation and words like "outhouse," "canceled," and "Ivan" floated over to our booth. The occasional finger pointed our way.

I reached for a napkin from the metal dispenser at the end of our table. "Do you hear the same pieces of conversation I do?" I asked Candie as I swiped barbeque sauce from my fingers.

Candie held up her pinkie finger in a gesture that she'd answer in a second after she swallowed her mouthful of sandwich. She patted her lips with a rumpled napkin then cleared her throat. "My ears are about to sizzle right off with all I'm hearing from the surrounding tables. But you know Wings Falls. Keeping a secret is a major undertaking in this town. I can imagine what the guys sitting in the barber chair at Clyde's barber shop are saying."

Clyde was Roberta Holden's husband. Roberta was a fellow Loopy Lady and reporter for the *Senior Chatter,* a weekly newsletter published by the Wings Falls Senior Center. She kept the town's seniors up-to-date on all that was happening, from the town's budget meeting to who had a new grandchild. She often said the men who climbed into Clyde's barber chair were worse gossips than any woman.

I laughed. "I'm sure you're right. I've often thought Hank should sit in one of the chairs in his barber shop, hide behind a newspaper, and listen to all the men talking. He'd solve his cases in no time."

Candie placed a hand over her mouth and started to cough. "I can just picture Hank sitting there with a pair of dark sunglasses on and a floppy hat pulled down over his forehead." She took a deep breath and waved her hand in front of her face.

I looked with concern at my cousin. "Are you all right? Do you want me to pound you on the back?"

"I'm fine, but I can't imagine your Hunky Hank being able to hide his identity for very long. He's too well known in Wings Falls." Candie swirled a sweet potato fry in the blob of ketchup on her plate then popped it into her mouth.

I brought up the image of my boyfriend Candie had described and laughed. Nope, that wasn't going to happen. Since Wings Falls Police Department lured him away from Albany PD a little more than a year ago, he'd established himself as the lead detective at the station and was well known around town as a great guy. Much to my chagrin at the time, Candie gave him the moniker of my Hunky Hank, which I was now happy that he was—all mine and certainly a hunk.

"What are you doing here with my nephew, you floozy?"

Our heads whipped around at the sound of the unhappy familiar voice.

CHAPTER FOURTEEN

———

I placed my sandwich on my plate and leaned out of our booth. Helen Garber stood next to a table in back of us with her hands on her ample hips, glaring down at its occupants. Her finger trembled with rage as she shook it at Sunny Foxx, who was sitting with none other than fireman Drew Ellis. Helen, in all her brilliant-colored glory, was not happy about the match. I wondered why.

"Did you know that fellow was Helen's nephew?" I asked Candie. She, too, along with most of the café, was craning her neck to watch the disturbance caused by Helen.

Candie swallowed the sweet potato fry she'd just taken a bite of and shook her head. "At Loopy Ladies, she never mentioned having any siblings, let alone a nephew."

I nodded. "Yeah, he didn't look familiar when I saw him yesterday, but he seemed to know Hank, so I asked him who he was. His name is Drew Ellis. He's new to the fire company, but Hank said he's had dealings with his father. It seems the father and Ivan didn't get along. Something about a boundary dispute between them. Sounded like silly kid stuff to me."

"It would depend upon where the land is situated. You know any property around here on the shores of Lake George could be worth into the millions."

Candie was right about that. Lakeside property was very valuable.

As I watched Helen, Sunny rose from her seat, donned her coat, and left Sweetie Pie's. Helen slid into the girl's empty seat. Drew looked far from happy with his aunt. She continued her harangue but now in a lowered voice so I couldn't hear what she said. I turned back to my meal. Most of it now resided in my very happy stomach. There were only a couple of sweet potato fries left, which I quickly devoured.

"Ladies, would you care for some dessert? I have an apple pie fresh out of the oven that Aaron baked."

I glanced over at Candie. "What do you say? I don't think we can pass up Franny's offer, especially since Aaron baked it. It'd be disloyal to Hank if I didn't try it."

Candie licked a spot of barbeque sauce from the corner of her mouth. "Oh, if you insist. We do have to support our youth's culinary endeavors."

I laughed. Aaron hoped to one day open his own restaurant after getting his culinary arts degree. After getting away from a gang he'd been hanging out with in Albany, he'd made a real turnaround with his life in the time he'd been here. His girlfriend, Joy, had been a major influence in this change. She also was going to the same college for a degree in culinary arts. Who knows. Maybe one day they'd open a restaurant together. One could always hope.

Ten minutes later, Candie was scraping her fork along her plate, trying to scoop up any remaining crumbs from her apple pie. "Aaron outdid himself with this pie. The crust was so flaky, it melted in my mouth."

"I agree. He certainly has become quite the chef since he started working here. Ready to head on home and see if you can patch up things between Mark and Dixie?" I asked, reaching for my coat and purse.

Candie did the same on her side of the booth. She shrugged into her coat. "At this point, I'll try anything." Candie's phone pinged. "That's Mark. He said he'd meet me at your house in about twenty minutes."

I glanced at my phone—no messages from Hank. If history repeated itself and this case resembled the other murder investigations he'd been involved with since moving here from Albany, our time together until it was solved would be limited. Hank was a devoted policeman and wouldn't rest until the murderer was found. Murders meant less Hank and me time. While I might become a bit jealous of sharing him with his job, I wouldn't change him in any way.

Evening had descended over Wings Falls by the time we left Sweetie Pie's. On the way out of the café, I waved goodbye to Franny and called a goodbye to Aaron and Joy, who were busy in the kitchen prepping food for the crowded restaurant. I noticed Helen had left, but her nephew was still seated, staring into a mug of coffee as if it would give him the answers to all his problems.

Once seated in my Bug, I turned to Candie and asked, "What do you think Helen was all about this evening? Why was she so upset seeing Drew with Sunny?"

Candie folded her hands over the purse she held on her lap. "Dang if I know. Other than being a flirt, I don't know a thing about this Sunny Foxx. Do you?"

I started my car and backed out of Sweetie Pie's parking lot. "I've never seen her, and Hank never said a word about her before she started clinging on to him at the Civic Center."

Candie buckled her seat belt and turned towards me. "I will say for once I agree with Helen. Sunny is quite the hussy. Where'd she come from?"

I shook my head. "All Hank said was she was the station commander's niece and she was working as his secretary while his regular secretary was out on maternity leave. I gather she's new to the job."

Candie tugged her hair from under the collar of her coat. "Humph. I'd keep an eye out for her. You know a man in uniform sends some girls' hearts a flutter."

"Well. I shouldn't have to worry about that. Hank doesn't wear a uniform to work. He's a plainclothes officer. Besides, I trust him."

It was a short drive to my house. Sure enough, when I pulled into my driveway, Mark's car was parked behind Hank's Jeep. "Let's go collect your fur babies so you can head home and start patching up Dixie and Mark's relationship."

Mark exited his car and approached my Bug. He must have stopped home on the way over to my house, as he no longer wore his costume from earlier in the day. His jeans and red-and-black-checked fleece jacket looked a lot warmer than his tights. He opened Candie's door so she could step out then gathered her into his arms and planted a very loving kiss on her lips. I smiled. I hoped it wouldn't take too much coaxing on Dixie's part to forgive Mark for taking Cuddles away.

"How are things going with Ivan's death?" I asked as I rounded my car.

"About as expected. Doc Cordone has officially stated his death as suspicious, so the police are handling it as a murder," Mark said, sliding an arm over Candie's shoulder.

"That means Hank will have a late night, I'm sure." Unfortunately, I was becoming used to this drill.

Mark nodded. "Yeah, I'm afraid so. He sent his love and asked if Nina could do a sleepover."

A funny thought entered my head, and I chuckled. "I hope Rob Anderson hasn't snapped any pictures of the crime scene with Hank as investigative officer. Can't you see Hank dressed as a court page on the front page of the *Tribune*?" Rob was a reporter for our local newspaper. I could imagine the razzing Hank would receive at the station if his picture dressed in tights made the local news. "Did he have to spend the day in his tights?"

Mark laughed, too. "No, when Hank realized it was going to be a long day, he got one of the guys to run him home so he could change."

A smile crept across Candie's face. "Oh, but think how sexy the picture would have been. You'd have half the North Country drooling over him."

True, I thought, his legs were sexy, along with the rest of him, but I didn't need other women lusting after him. Sunny had been enough. "No, thanks. I don't need that dilemma. You two gather up your pets and get on home. See you tomorrow at Loopy Ladies, Candie?"

With her pets loaded into their car, I waved from my doorway as they pulled out of my driveway. I walked into my house and an empty living room. Well, empty except for Porkchop, Nina, and me. "Okay, pups, I guess it's the three of us tonight. Hank is busy and won't be able to join us."

Another murder. Another lonely night. Dating Hank wasn't easy. No wonder the divorce rate among law enforcement officers was so high.

CHAPTER FIFTEEN

―――――

I curled up on the sofa in my living room and covered myself with the red and white afghan Memaw Parker had crocheted for my eighteenth birthday. Porkchop and Nina resumed their sleeping positions curled in front of the fireplace.

"Porkchop, stop it." I swatted at what I thought was my dog tugging at my curly brown hair.

"Nope, Sleeping Beauty, it's not Porkie. Just your friendly neighborhood policeman."

My eyes flew open. Hank was tucking a stray curl behind my ears. He leaned in and kissed me. Now I was fully awake. I sat up and pulled him towards me. "What time is it?" I squinted at the schoolhouse clock that hung on the wall across from me. "Is the time correct? Two o'clock?"

Hank glanced over at the clock. "Yep. I know it's late, but I needed to see you. Hope you don't mind the hour."

Now that Hank and I were a steady couple, I had given him a key to my house. Since I usually knew his comings and goings, he didn't use it often, but after a day like today, I was glad he had. With him next to me, my world was right again.

Porkchop and Nina raised their heads from their beds. Their tails began to wag, and they barked with excitement. They both stood and bounded towards Hank. He bent and patted the yipping dogs.

I swung my legs onto the floor and rose from the sofa. "We'd better let them out to do their business. Then maybe they'll settle back down. I know it's late, but would you like something to eat? I bet you didn't have dinner." I knew once Hank was involved in a case, all thoughts of food flew out of his mind.

Hank patted his leg for Nina to follow him. I did the same for Porkchop. We walked into my kitchen, where I switched on the outside light, opened the back door, and scooted the dogs out into my fenced backyard. I opened the refrigerator door and peered into its stark interior. Unlike Aaron, I wasn't known for my culinary skills. A slice of three-day-old pizza in a ziplock bag lay on the top shelf next to a bag of sesame seed bagels and a pound of bacon. In the door, I did keep a supply of Hank's favorite beer, Trails Head. He stood behind me and scanned the meager contents. "I grabbed a burger from the fast-food joint in town earlier this evening. I'm fine. What I want right now is to drink in your warmth."

From the heat flooding through me, he'd get plenty of it. I turned into his arms and pressed myself against him then pulled his head down and kissed him with all of my love. Scratching at the back door distracted me. I ran a finger over his lips. "Don't move. I'll be right back."

Hank chuckled and swatted my rear as I pulled away to let the dogs in. "I'll be waiting for you."

After I fed each dog a treat, they settled back onto their beds. Hank stood in the doorway to the kitchen. I walked over and took his strong hand in mine. "Now it's time for us," I said, leading him down the hall to my bedroom. I flipped on the overhead light to my childhood bedroom. At least I had finally taken down the Donnie Osmond poster that once stared down at us. The bed was now a roomy queen size covered with a soft gray comforter. I pulled back the covers and slid under them. Hank removed his clothes and did the same. I laid my head on his muscled chest and listened to his strong heartbeat. I glanced up at him. "Do you want to talk about today?"

"There's not much to say other than Doc Cordone confirmed Ivan didn't die of natural causes. Now, we just have to figure out who disliked him enough to want to do him in."

I thought of the people who I'd seen yesterday who could fit into a murderer category—Jim Turner, Helen Garber, Drew Ellis, Martha Callaway, Sunny Foxx with the two x's, or the unknown fellow from the dance. Could it be one of them or someone else altogether?

I ran a finger through the brown curls on his chest. "You'll find who killed him. You always do."

He placed a hand over mine to still my actions. "Uh hum. Let's talk about something else, like this." He leaned down and kissed me.

* * *

I stirred in my bed and reached over for Hank and found only rumpled blankets. My eyes snapped open. The bed was empty, except for me, of course. Where was he? I threw back my covers and grabbed my robe from the bottom of the bed. I slipped on fleece-lined slippers then shuffled into the kitchen. Hank stood by the stove, frying up bacon. He had tied one of my aprons around his waist. A lightly toasted bagel lay on a plate on the counter. Coffee brewed in the coffeepot. Its aroma tickled my nose.

Porkchop and Nina sat at his feet, hoping for a piece of bacon to drop their way. I tiptoed up behind him and encircled his waist with my arms. "Hey, handsome. Do I know you?"

Hank jerked in surprise. He chuckled and turned towards me. "Make a noise next time. I could have done serious damage to myself."

"I like your new look," I said, pointing to the apron he'd tied over his boxers.

He stepped back and struck a modeling pose. "Anything to please my lady."

I blushed, thinking about last night. "Oh, you pleased me all right." I glanced at the digital clock on my microwave—6:45. "Do you need to get to the station soon?"

Hank turned back to the stove to flip the bacon. "Unfortunately, yes. I'll stop home first for a shower and a change of clothes."

I reached down and scratched both dogs between the ears. They were still standing guard over the bacon. "Do you want Nina to spend the day?"

"No. I know you'll stop at Loopy Ladies today to gossip with your lady friends. I'll drop her off at For Pet's Sake for some doggie day care."

I poked him in the ribs. "It's not all gossiping. We do some productive rug hooking, too."

"Uh-huh," he said, placing the cooked bacon on a paper towel to drain. "Ready to eat?"

* * *

I couldn't help myself. I raised my hand to my mouth to stifle another yawn. Last night with Hank was wonderful, but I was paying for my lack of sleep now.

Candie leaned over her hooking and whispered into my ear, "Either Porkchop and Nina didn't settle down after I left last night, or Hank stopped over. Which is it?"

A smile tugged at my lips as I remembered last night. "The second one."

We, along with the other Loopy Ladies, were seated around the large oak table in Lucy Foster's hooking room at The Ewe and Me. Porkchop was curled at my feet, chewing on the rawhide bone Lucy's husband, Ralph, had given him this morning. Ralph spoiled Porkchop something fierce, proclaiming him the official "shop dog." Porkchop lapped up the attention. Although, he wasn't the only dog to accompany their owner on Monday mornings to our hooking sessions. Patsy Ikeda often brought her beautiful Japanese Spitz, Hana, along with her.

I placed a finger to my lips and glanced around the table at the ladies busy hooking and talking. "Shhh. I don't want all of Wings Falls knowing what I do."

Candie leaned back in her chair and laughed. "With Gladys O'Malley as your neighbor, good luck. Especially, since she's Hank's aunt."

Gladys's head whipped around towards us. "Did I hear you mention Hank's name? I saw the light on in your house early this morning. Oh, not that I was looking. I was on my way to the bathroom and saw a light shining through your window."

Candie folded her arms across her chest. A smug look appeared on her face. "See? I told you she'd know."

I nudged her foot under the table. She thought she was such a smartie pants.

Gladys was still in her Saint Patrick's Day mode. Today, she'd donned a green cable knit sweater the same bright color of her curls. "What did my nephew have to say about that poor Ivan Kline?"

A choking sound came from the end of the table. I looked over to see Jane Burrows holding a napkin in front of her mouth. Susan Mayfield was pounding her on the back to help her catch her breath.

What had brought that on?

CHAPTER SIXTEEN

———

Why would the mention of Ivan Kline upset Jane? That was a mystery for Hank to unravel. I wasn't going to get involved in another murder investigation. I shook my head and smoothed my rug over the frame before reaching for a strip of red wool for the flag in my rug. I was looking forward to summer and hooking a small rug featuring a crow perched on a slice of watermelon. An American flag rested in its beak.

"Let me get you a bottle of water from the back," Lucy said to Jane, rising from her chair.

Water bottles. That triggered a memory from yesterday morning. Why were they on the ground near our outhouse yesterday morning? I know the guys wouldn't have left them there when they delivered the outhouse. I leaned over my frame and let out a sigh as I started to pull loops.

"What's bothering you? You act like you have the weight of the world on your shoulders," Candie said as she stretched rug hooking linen, with a pattern featuring a bee skep, a wicker basket where bees made their home, with a crow perched on top drawn on it, over her frame. She, also, was anticipating summer.

"When Lucy mentioned getting Jane a water bottle, it brought to mind the ones strewn on the ground near our outhouse. Don't you think it was strange they were there?"

Candie tapped her rug hook against her chin. "Now that you mention it, I do. Why would anyone be having a drink outside in this cold weather? It would be an icicle before it hit your lips."

My eyes widened. "Doc Cordone said that Ivan died of hypothermia. What if the murderer dumped the contents of those bottles of water on Ivan? Did you notice the icicles that had formed on his uniform jacket, his hair and eyelids? I would think he would have put up a fuss if such a thing happened."

Candie shivered at my description of Ivan. "Yeah, you would think so."

A thought struck me, and I sat up straighter in my chair. "Unless he was too drunk to fight off the murderer."

Candie pursed her Passion Pink–covered lips. "Yes, or maybe he was passed out."

I stared down at my rug, unable to fathom how someone could do such a thing. "Who would have left him there to freeze to death? I don't know of anyone that would be so cruel."

"Sugar, I can't think of such a soul either. Let's put poor Ivan out of our minds for a while and enjoy our rug hooking."

I wished that could have been the plan for the morning, but Gladys was like Porkchop with his bone and wouldn't let go.

"Missy, you didn't answer my question. What did my nephew have to say about Ivan's demise?"

All heads swiveled towards me. I glanced up from my hooking. "Nothing."

"What do you mean nothing? Surely, he mentioned something."

I shook my head. Gladys wouldn't let it go. "I'm sorry to disappoint you, but he was bone-tired when he arrived at my house and said very little about Ivan's death, other than Doc Cordone felt he didn't die of natural causes."

"Humph. Well, I hope they solve this crime soon so we can have the outhouse races. I still need to win my regal title." Gladys lifted her chin in a queenly manner and patted her curls.

"Gladys!" Anita Plum said in what sounded like her best school teacher voice. "A man has passed away. Have some respect."

"He never showed my brother any respect," Helen Garber said from the end of the table. All hooking stopped. She had the group's full attention. She certainly wasn't displaying any compassion for Ivan's passing. I noted once again she'd mentioned a brother, something she had never done before, and wondered if there had been a family rift at one time. Was it the reason why we didn't know about him?

CHAPTER SEVENTEEN

_____

"Stop evading my question. What did Hank say last night about Ivan?" Gladys asked.

I glanced around the table and squirmed in my seat. All eyes were fixed on me. Since I dated the town's lead detective, the ladies thought I was the go-to source for anything police- related. I hated to disappoint them, but Hank hadn't shared his findings with me. Even if he did, I wouldn't blab them far and wide. I'd never betray his confidence. The ladies would have to rely on what they read in the *Tribune* for any updates on Ivan's death.

"Yes, Hank stopped over, but he was exhausted from a long day of work. He basically gave Nina a scratch and went to sleep." They didn't need to know it was in my bed.

Gladys raised an eyebrow then glanced around the room. "Humph. Does she think we were all born yesterday?"

Heads nodded in response to her question.

I felt my cheeks heat up and sent a death glare towards Candie. She shrugged her shoulders and mouthed, *What?*

"Don't go acting all innocent with me. You started this."

I turned back to the group. "Honestly, ladies, you all know as much as I do about Ivan's demise."

"If you say so," Gladys mumbled as she jabbed her hook into her pattern of a leaping rabbit surrounded by colorful Easter eggs.

"Are we still on for your book signing and reading tomorrow afternoon?"

Jane Burrows had asked Porkchop and me to come to the library tomorrow. Before my book was even published, she wanted to schedule me to read my children's book, *Porkchop the Wonder Dog,* to a group of preschoolers who met at the library in the afternoon. I appreciated her support and was thrilled to do the reading. I had been busy promoting and selling my book since it was released. This was a long-awaited dream of mine to be a published author, and thanks to Bob Spellman at Rolling Brook Press, it had come true. Now, I was busier than I could have ever imagined.

"Porkchop and I just have to pick out the outfit he's going to wear for the children, and then we're ready," I said, doing a mental inventory of his outfits I had stored in a bin at home. Should he come as a pirate, cowboy, or make it a formal event and wear his tuxedo? Nope, this was going to be a surprise for the adults and kids alike attending Porkchop's big event.

"Right, Porkchop?" I asked as I glanced under the table to find him still busy working on the bone Ralph gave him.

All the ladies laughed, except for Candie. Her lips formed into a pout.

"I'll be there with Robby and Molly. I know they'll love your story, and Porkchop will be a hit, too. Make sure you save two books for me and autograph them for my kids," Susan Mayfield said.

Susan's two children were the perfect age for my book, preschoolers.

"Thanks, Susan. I'll sign them tonight so I don't forget. I appreciate it."

"You and Hank have supported our business, and it's time to return the favor." Susan was referring to Momma Mia's, the restaurant she owned with her husband Brian.

"You're going to be busy tomorrow afternoon?" Candie's voice sounded whinier than one of the children missing their nap that Porkchop and I were going to entertain tomorrow.

I laid my hook on the table and turned to my cousin. "What's the matter? You knew once my book was released, I'd be doing book signings and events. Aren't you happy for me?"

She rubbed a finger over the tear forming on the tip of her long eyelashes. Luckily, the other ladies were so absorbed with their hooking and gabbing with each other, they didn't notice Candie's distress.

I reached over and touched her pale hand. "Honey, what's the matter? Is it this situation with Dixie and Mark?

Candie shook her head. "No, I work in the morning tomorrow and have the afternoon off. I thought maybe we could hang out together. You know, since Mark will be working and I'm sure Hank will be busy."

"How's your latest book coming?" I asked, mentioning the latest steamy book she was writing. I thought this would brighten her mood. She was always happy to share her progress with the Loopy Ladies, often asking their advice on a particular plot point. They loved knowing they had a hand in helping Candie write her books.

Candie picked up a wool strip and her hook and pulled a loop through the rug backing. She shrugged her shoulders. "Okay, I guess. There's not much romance in paradise right now. I think I have writer's block."

My eyes widened. For Candie not to be able to have panting studs and heaving breasts flowing out of the tips of her fingers was a major sign something was wrong. She was a master of all things romantic.

I placed my hand over hers. She looked up at me with her sad violet eyes. "Come with me tomorrow. I could use your help."

She let out a deep sigh. "If you say so."

I laughed. "You know all the experience I've had with young kids… Nil. Hopefully, the moms will keep their young ones in line, but I could use the extra eyes, ears, and hands."

Candie gave me a weak smile. "Okay, I'll come over after work. I'll need to stop home first to tend to Dixie and Annie."

"Sounds like a plan." I glanced at my Timex watch, seeing that it was eleven thirty. "Geez, these two hours have flown by. I think I'll pack up and stop at Shop and Save for a couple of sandwiches. Knowing Hank, he's probably going to skip lunch. He does that when he's involved with a case. I'll surprise him with a mini picnic in his office."

Candie started to pack up her rug hooking, too. "Ahh, that's sweet. I'd better get over to City Hall if I don't want to get fired."

I laughed. "Yeah, like you don't have an in with the mayor."

"True, but I don't want to take advantage of that. It would reflect badly on Mark."

I poked my head under the table. Porkchop lay with his head on his paws, snoozing. He had finished off his bone. I stroked his head. "Come on, Porkie. I know you've had such a rough morning. It's time for us to go." He stirred as I clipped on his leash.

I straightened up and stuffed my frame, rug, hook, scissors, and wool strips into the red canvas bag I used to lug all my rug hooking goodies. Rug hookers didn't travel light.

Candie stood and slipped on her jacket. I did the same. I was looking forward to the day when we could pack away all this winter gear and go outside with just a light sweater or none at all.

Porkchop stretched his long reddish-brown body as I gently tugged on his leash to follow me. I turned and waved to the Loopy Ladies, some of whom were packing up, too.

"Bye, everyone. Have a great rest of your day."

Goodbyes and well wishes followed me out of The Ewe.

Candie's Precious was parked next to my Bug. When we got to my car, she leaned over and hugged me. "Okay, sweetie. I'll talk to you this evening if you're not busy with Hank." She gave me a sassy wink.

"Oh, you. Say hi to Mark for me," I said, opening the car door to stow my bag in the back. Porkchop jumped onto the front seat, circled the cushion, and then curled up and snuggled in.

I pulled out of my parking space, honked, and waved to Candie. I pointed the Bug in the direction of home. I wanted to drop off Porkchop before I headed to the Shop and Save for my surprise lunch picnic. Little did I know…I was the one getting the surprise.

CHAPTER EIGHTEEN

―――――

"Hi, Sam. What can I do for you today?"

The Shop and Save was not your ordinary grocery store. Sure, they had all the usual items you'd expect from a large supermarket, but their deli department was to die for. They not only sliced lunchmeat and cheese to order, but they'd also fashion your pick into mouthwatering sandwiches. You could add delicious freshly made pasta and potato salads to your order, too.

"Hi, Rita. Two roast beef and Swiss cheese sandwiches on rye plus two pasta salads to go with them, please." I had gone to Wings Falls High with Rita Bolster. She started at the Shop and Save right after graduation as a stock girl. Now she was the manager of the deli department. Her purple-dyed hair was tucked into a hairnet. A white apron sporting the store's logo was tied around her waist. A smile was spread across her friendly face.

"Coming right up. Having lunch with someone special?" It was no secret, especially in a town the size of Wings Falls, that I dated Hank.

"Yeah, I thought I'd surprise Hank. He's probably too wrapped up in his latest case and will forget to eat."

Rita looked up from the meat slicer. "That's right. I heard someone was killed at the staging area for the outhouse races. Do the police have any idea who did it?"

I shook my head. "Not that I know of."

"Such a shame. I hope they find the murderer soon. It almost makes me nervous to leave my house and come to work. But this happened in Lake George and not Wings Falls, right?" Rita finished slicing the cheese and roast beef and started to assemble the sandwiches.

"Yes, but Chief Kelly asked Wings Falls to help since they are down quite a few officers because of the flu." I really didn't want to talk about the murder. Thankfully, another couple stood in back of me waiting for service. This prodded Rita to concentrate on my order. She finished wrapping the sandwiches and scooped out two pasta salads into plastic containers, priced my order, and then handed it over the counter to me.

I placed the food into the small shopping basket I'd slung over my arm. "Thanks, Rita. The sandwiches and pasta salads look really tasty. My mouth is watering for a bite of them."

"Enjoy. See you next time you're in." She turned to the couple waiting behind me and asked them what they would like.

*   *   *

It was only a short ten-minute drive from the Shop and Save to the Wings Fall Police station. I pulled the Bug into the space designated for visitors next to a black and white cruiser. I reached over to the passenger seat for my brown C-patterned Coach purse and the shopping bag containing the surprise lunch for Hank and myself. In my mind's eye, I could see the smile of appreciation spread across his face when I showed him what I brought. True, since he was at work he couldn't "properly" show his gratitude for my feeding him, but I knew he'd make up for it later when he, hopefully, stopped by my house.

I walked up the cement steps of the square brick building that housed the police force and was startled when the metal front door suddenly swung open. Barreling out was Joe Peters. I stepped back so he wouldn't knock me down. I plastered a smile on my face. "Hi, Joe."

His unibrow furrowed as he stopped short at my greeting. "*Humph.*"

I guess that was better than "You're under arrest and we're throwing away the key," which was what I knew he'd love to say to me sooner rather than later.

I kept my smile in place, as difficult as it was for me to do, and took the high road. "How's Portia and her new store doing?" Portia was Joe's wife. I recently referred to her business as a consignment store, only to have her correct me. She informed me, rather huffily I might say, that it was a boutique for women looking for upscale clothing treasures.

"Fine," he grunted. "I'm busy." He hurried down the steps.

"Tell her to give me a call if she ever gets any designer purses in," I called after him as he pulled open the door on a cruiser.

He didn't bother to answer me back.

I shrugged my shoulders and pulled open the heavy metal door of the station.

I walked over to the front desk. The station's PCO, public communications officer, Wanda Thurston, was busy speaking into the headset nestled amongst her black curly hair. She held up a finger. Her full red-lipstick-colored lips mouthed, *One minute.*

I nodded and took a seat on one of the hard metal chairs lining the reception area's walls. I placed the shopping bag containing Hank's and my surprise lunch at my feet on the brown and tan tiled floor and glanced around the room. Pictures of the governor and the station commander hung on the paneled wall across from me. American and New York State flags stood in the corner.

"Hi, Sam," Wanda called from behind the bulletproof glass that separated her from the general public.

I grabbed my shopping bag from the floor, stood, and walked over to her. I spoke through the small hole cut into the glass. "Hi, Wanda. I thought I'd surprise Hank with some lunch. I know he doesn't always take time out to eat when he's busy with a case."

Wanda nodded. "Sure, I'll buzz you through." She pushed a button on the console in front of her, and the lock on the door separating the main workings of the station from the public area clicked open.

"Thanks," I said and pulled the heavy door open.

"Enjoy your lunch," she called after me.

The hub of the station was a hive of activity. Officers sat behind metal desks either talking on phones, typing on their computers, or speaking to each other. I wondered how many of them were involved with solving Ivan Kline's murder. I waved to Officer Reed as I walked past his desk. He nodded a greeting in return.

After dating Hank for over a year now and having visited him many times at the station, I knew the way to his office. I walked down a short hallway to the end and raised my hand to knock on the door. I noticed it was slightly open and heard voices from the other side. More like a male voice and a woman crying.

I nudged the door open and blinked. I couldn't believe the scene unfolding before me. Hank stood next to his desk with his arms around Sunny Foxx, of the two x's fame. She was crying on his shoulder. I cleared my throat, as I was certain they weren't aware of my presence.

Startled, Sunny backed away from Hank. His face blazed a bright red.

Hank took a step towards me. "Sam, it's not what you think. Let me explain."

I backed up from him. My mind was reeling from what I had walked in on. Hank, my Hank, in another woman's arms? No, it couldn't be. Maybe, if I stepped out of his office and came in again, I'd see him behind his state-issued metal desk. He'd be hard at work trying to solve Ivan Kline's murder. His hair would be mussed, and the cute brown curl that refused to stay in place would be resting on his forehead. One of the cartoon-figured ties he loved to wear would be hanging loose around his neck.

I shook my head. Nope, the reality was much different from what I imagined. I walked over to his desk and dumped out the sandwiches and pasta salad onto the paperwork scattered on top. The lid to one of the pasta salads flipped open, and I didn't give a fig if the mayo and noodle salads spilling out were on an important document or not. I turned to Hank, whose mouth hung open, and pointed to a sniveling Sunny. "I hope you and she enjoy your lunch." I turned and walked out of his office. Tears threatened to stream down my face, but I bit the inside of my mouth to stem the flow. Nobody, and I mean nobody, was going to see me cry, not over a man. Never again. I'd learned that hard lesson from my ex, George, and wasn't about to repeat it.

CHAPTER NINETEEN

———

"I swear, Porkchop, you are the only man I want in my life now and forever. We won't be seeing your buddy Hank anymore." I refused to cry over the scene I'd walked in on in Hank's office. I still hadn't shed a tear, and I wasn't going to. I sat on my sofa with Porkchop cuddled on my lap. My phone rang for about the one hundredth time since I'd arrived home after I'd pulled out of the Wings Falls Police station's parking lot about an hour ago. I checked the caller ID, and like all the other calls, it was from Hank. I refused to answer it.

Maybe I was being pigheaded and a wee bit childish, but I'd never forget the morning George asked me for a divorce, from what I had thought was a loving and caring twenty-five-year marriage. He wanted to marry the secretary of the funeral business we co-owned together. Apparently, his late-night body pickups involved one very live body.

Porkchop raised his small head and looked at me with his chocolate-brown eyes. He started to whine at the mention of Hank's name. He'd miss Hank and Nina as much as I would, but as I'd learned over the years, such was life. I'd hurt for a while, but hopefully sooner rather than later, the pain would lessen. And here I'd thought Porkchop was such a good judge of character. He'd never taken to George but loved Hank from the very beginning. Oh, well. We could all make mistakes, even my loving pup.

A glance at the clock showed that it was three pm. I pushed myself off the sofa. "Okay, Porkie, let's find something to eat." I'd left what was going to be my lunch in Hank's office and hadn't eaten since I returned home. My stomach had churned too much to give eating a thought. Now it sent out a growl of hunger.

Porkchop trotted next to me into the kitchen. "Okay, you first. You're easy." I reached down for his bone-shaped bowl and poured a handful of kibble into it. "Now let's see what's in the refrigerator for me." Not much had changed from the morning. I pulled out the bag of sesame seed bagels and popped one into the toaster then filled the kettle on the stove to boil water for a mug of tea.

With my tea and bagel in hand, I retreated to the den. I still had to arrange things for tomorrow's book reading at the library. I knew the costume Porkchop would wear, but I needed to make sure I had pens and copies of my books packed for the signing at the library.

My phone rang again. This time the caller ID read Candie's name. "Hi, Candie, what's up?"

"Don't 'Hi, Candie, what's up,' me. Hank called me. He's frantic. He said he's been trying to call you, but you won't pick up. He'd be over, but he can't leave the station right now, what with the murder investigation."

"Is that the excuse he gave you? I guess it's as good as any, not that I want to see him."

"I'm leaving City Hall right now and will be at your place in ten minutes. Don't you dare go anywhere, if you know what's good for you." Candie disconnected, not giving me a chance to reply.

I looked down at Porkchop. He lay curled up next to me amongst the costumes I'd spread over the cushions of the loveseat in my den. "Your aunt Candie is on her way over. Remember, Porkie, stiff upper lip. No crying over what happened in Hank's office." I swiped at a lone tear threatening to trickle down my cheek. I reached over to my CD player and punched the On button. It still held my Roy Orbison CD. He and Elvis tied for my all-time favorite singers. I guess I was an old soul. The young people could keep their Taylor Swift and company. I laid my head back against the sofa and drank in Roy's mellow voice. The tension of today began to seep out of my body as I listened to the lyrics. Porkchop nuzzled his head under my hand. He always knew when I needed comforting. My eyes drifted shut.

My front door slammed open. I jerked up in my seat. Porkchop jumped off the loveseat and trotted into the living room. "Sam? Sam, where are you? You'd better have a good excuse as to why you aren't picking up Hank's phone calls. If not, like Memaw used to say, 'I'm taking you to the woodshed for a good talking to with a hickory switch.'"

In spite of all that had happened today, a smile twitched at my lips. I loved my dear cousin's Southern sense of humor. "I'm in the den," I called out to her. I stood and walked to the den door.

Candie tossed her bejeweled purse on the desk that sat across from the loveseat then tugged off her wool gloves. Her coat followed as she tossed it on top of the desk. She stood before me with her hands on her hips, tapping the tip of her pink cowboy boots. "All right, missy, you have some explaining to do. What's with all this nonsense of not answering Hank's phone calls? I want the whole lowdown. Don't you dare leave anything out."

I punched the CD player off then sat back down on the loveseat. From the tone of her voice, as I looked up at her towering over me and the expression on her smooth face, I knew she meant business. "Remember at The Ewe, I mentioned stopping at Shop and Save and buying lunch for Hank and me?"

Candie waggled her fingers for me to speed up my story. "Soooo?"

"Sooo, I had Rita Bolster put together a roast beef sandwich and pasta salad lunch I knew he'd love. When I got to the police station, Wanda buzzed me right through to Hank's office. I was excited to surprise him, only I was the one to get the surprise."

Candie pushed aside the costumes spread out on the loveseat and sat down next to me. Porkchop jumped at my legs, so I reached down and picked him up. I settled him on my lap and idly stroked the top of his head.

Candie's eyes widened. "What kind of a surprise? When Hank called my phone, he didn't mention a surprise, only that it was urgent to speak to you. He said you misunderstood something, and he couldn't leave the station yet."

"Oh, I didn't misunderstand a thing. When I walked into his office, Sunny Foxx was nestled in his arms, crying her little eyes out. You remember her from this past weekend at the Firemen's Convention. First, she was hanging all over Hank, and then at the dance she was clinging to Ivan Kline."

Candie's mouth dropped open. "I don't believe it. Not Hank."

I pointed to my eyes. "These eyes don't lie. I know what I saw, and I won't be fooled again, like I was with George. Right, Porkchop? It's just you and me from now on." He stirred in my lap.

Candie reached over and placed her slim hand over mine. "Sam, don't judge Hank too harshly. There are things about this Ivan Kline murder case that I can't explain right now, but what I do know is that Hank loves you with all of his heart and he'd never betray you like that tom cat you were married to."

"I was burnt badly once by my ex George. I'm not going to let that happen again. I made it fine on my own before Hank moved here and I can do it again."

Candie shifted uncomfortably on the loveseat's cushion. I could tell she was holding back something from me. We were closer than sisters and could practically read each other's minds and moods. I could feel she wanted to tell me more.

"Sam, I can't. It's something I heard at my office. You know that since Mark is mayor, the police keep him updated on what is going on with the investigation. Just believe me when I tell you, Hank wouldn't betray you."

I shrugged my shoulders. "After my track record with men, I'm a little wary."

Candie squeezed my hand. "I know you are, darling, and for good reason, too. But you have a winner in Hank and don't have to worry about him. I'd better get home. I left the office in a bit of a hurry."

Candie stood and leaned over and kissed my cheek. "Patience, sweetheart. Patience. All will work out. I'll see myself out. You sit here with Porkchop and listen to some more Roy. He'll soothe your soul." She walked over to my desk and grabbed the coat and purse she had tossed there earlier.

"I love you," I called to her retreating back then leaned over and punched on my CD player.

She waved goodbye over her shoulder.

I heard the front door open and then a voice I wasn't prepared for. "How is she?"

I couldn't make out Candie's muffled response.

CHAPTER TWENTY

———

I sat with my back rigid against the loveseat, my resolve not to cry in place. Porkchop ran over to Hank. His tail wagged in greeting—Porkchop's that is. My pup flopped on his back and wiggled back and forth on the rug. Hank bent and scratched his belly. Before today, this display of affection between the two of them would have brought a smile to my face and warmed my heart. Now, I only felt sadness, knowing it was all coming to an end.

Hank looked up at me. "Can we talk about what happened in my office?"

I shrugged my shoulders. "What's there to talk about? I know what I saw. Sunny was wrapped in your arms."

"Sam, please listen to me. I swear it's not what it looks like." He held one of his strong hands out to me, pleading. My resolve to remain strong started to soften as I looked into his crystal-blue eyes. There stood the man who I loved unconditionally with all my heart. Should I listen to him, or would I be duped again like I was with my ex? I didn't know if I could stand such heartache once again.

Hank walked over to the wing chair that sat across the room from the loveseat. He turned to me and pointed to the chair. "May I?"

I nodded. He was here, so I might as well listen to his excuse for betraying me. Candie would have my hide if I didn't at least hear him out. Roy was crooning "In Dreams" as I watched Hank settle himself in the chair. How often I had dreamed of this handsome man sitting across from me. I shook myself to remember how I'd felt this afternoon. Now, I was living a nightmare.

Hank sat with his shoulders slumped. His hands dangled between his knees. He glanced up at me. "Sam, you are the only woman in my life. There is nothing between Sunny and me, other than a professional relationship."

My eyebrows rose at that one. "What profession is she in—throwing herself at men? Is she that kind of hooker? And I don't mean like the Loopy Ladies."

Hank's lips twitched into a smile. "No, she's not a lady of the streets. As I told you, she's the station commander's niece and working as his secretary, temporarily, while his real secretary is out on maternity leave. Apparently, though, Sunny comes with a lot of baggage. I can't tell you all the details, but her flirting has gotten her into some trouble with men before, but this time it's more serious, and we think it may be tied in with Ivan's murder."

I was shocked at Hank's revelation. "Ivan's murder? Did she kill him?"

"If I believed she had, she'd be under arrest right now, but I think she knows who did but won't tell me. What you walked in on was her trying to cry her way out of my questioning her about her past boyfriends. She's afraid one of them might kill her if she rats him out. Especially her soon-to-be ex-husband."

My eyes widened in surprise. "You mean she's married?"

Hank nodded. "From what she says, her divorce is almost final."

I remembered seeing the stranger at the dance talking to Sunny. He looked upset with her. Was he stalking her?

I mentioned my suspicions to Hank.

"Yeah, we're trying to check him out, but Sunny is too scared to reveal his whereabouts to me. Seems the guy did a really good number on her mind."

Now I felt sorry for Sunny. Women could get sucked into abusive relationships and not know how to get out. Hopefully, she'd found the help she needed to escape it.

"Hank, did you notice there were a number of other people who had issues with Ivan? Maybe they could have been involved with his murder."

He sat up straighter in the wing chair. "Yes, I did, but this is none of your business. I don't want you involved in his murder."

My jaw jutted out. He knew I didn't like being told what to or not to do. The CD started to play "I Drove All Night," one of my favorite Roy Orbison songs.

Hank rose from the chair and held his hand out to me. "Will you dance with me?"

I took his hand and was folded into his arms. We swayed back and forth to the sweet lyrics of the song.

"Sam, I would never cheat on you. Please believe me." He reached between us and touched the gold heart locket he'd given me last summer at Candie and Mark's wedding. "Remember what the initials stand for that I had engraved on the back of this heart? MTYLTT?"

I nodded. "More than yesterday, less than tomorrow."

"That's how much I love you, Sam. Please never forget it. I'll love you always and forever."

My resolve not to cry dissolved as tears streamed down my face. "I love you so much it scares me. I think I'd die if I ever lost you."

With his thumb, he brushed away my tears. "I feel the same way, sweetheart. I couldn't go on living without you." He leaned down. His lips met mine with a soul-searing kiss.

I took his hand and led him over to the end table. I punched the CD player to off then led him down the hall to my bedroom. He didn't know it, but I was determined he'd remain in my dreams without any interference from Miss Sunny Foxx with two x's, so I needed to find Ivan's murderer before she thought she could use Hank's shoulder to cry on again.

*　*　*

"Well, look who's here. Hi, Sam, and is this Porkchop the Wonder Dog?"

Penny Richards stood behind the reception desk of the town's library. I had babysat her years ago, as she kindly reminded me a few months back. When I had stopped in the library, she'd said hi to me, and I'd given her a blank look of recognition. She'd moved back to Wings Falls and now worked in the library. She was petite, barely reaching five feet. Long blonde waves cascaded over her slim shoulders. Even as a child, she had a love of books. She'd have a stack of her favorites waiting for me when I came over to babysit her. Her favorites, and I must say mine too, were Denys Cazet's Minnie and Moo series. We'd giggle for hours over the adventures of those two cows. Now, I thought, she had the perfect job, working as Jane Burrows' assistant in the children's section of the library. Jane was the head of the department. When I told the Loopy Ladies about my publishing success, Jane asked me to do a book signing and reading. So here I was with a canvas bag full of my books and Porkchop straining on his leash.

"Hi, Penny. Yep, the one and only. He's ready to strut his stuff. Right, Porkie?" I leaned down and ruffled his ears.

Penny smiled at Porkchop. "He sure is a cutie. The children will love him. Come on and follow me. I'll show you where we have you set up for your reading. Here, let me take that bag from you. It does look like Porkchop is ready and raring for the kids."

"Thank you. It would be a big help," I said, handing over the canvas bag to her. It was heavy. "I'll hold on to this." I held up the plastic bag containing his costume.

On the way to the room set up for my book signing, we passed Jane's office. I stopped at the door. "I'll catch up with you, Penny. I want to say hi to Jane."

"Okay, I'll place this bag in the second room to your right." She pointed to a glassed-in area a little farther down the aisle.

Jane's door was open, and she was on the phone. Her back was to me. By the agitated tone of her voice, she clearly was not happy with whoever was on the other end. "Jim, that incident with his brother happened years ago. The police aren't going to think you killed Ivan because of a teenage stunt gone wrong."

Was she talking to Jim Turner? And why would he think he was a suspect in Ivan's murder? Had he been in trouble with the law when he was younger? Ivan had made a reference to firecrackers and his brother when he passed by our table on Saturday night. As I remembered it, Jim wasn't very happy with Ivan's comment.

I backed out to continue down the aisle and give Jane some privacy with her conversation but accidently stepped on poor Porkchop's paw. Jane swiveled around in her chair, a look of surprise on her face.

"I need to go," she said into the phone and quickly hung up.

CHAPTER TWENTY-ONE

———

Jane stood and walked over to me. She glanced at her watch. "Hi, Sam. I'm glad you're early. It gives you plenty of time to set up and relax before your big event."

"Sorry, I didn't mean to interrupt your phone call. Were you talking to Jim?"

"Ummm, yes. He's coming over for dinner tonight, and I wanted to know if there was anything special he'd like me to make." Dating Jim was a new experience for her but one I hoped led to a long-term and happy relationship.

"I couldn't help but overhear you mention Ivan and his murder. On Saturday night, Jim looked upset with Ivan when he mentioned firecrackers and his brother. Did they have a past history together?"

Jane ran a trembling hand through her cropped, gray-streaked brown hair. "Of course not. They only know each other through the fire departments. You know, since they're both fire chiefs."

She tugged at the hem of her navy sweater set she'd paired with khaki slacks today. Sweater sets and khaki slacks were hers and her mother's clothing options of choice. "Come on, let's get you set up." She closed her office door and led me to the room Penny had mentioned earlier, ending any further discussion concerning Jim Turner.

As I looked at Porkchop, I wondered if she was hiding something about Jim's past that had a bearing on Ivan's murder. And why had Ivan mentioned his brother? Had Jim and Ivan's brother been friends? Was there a riff between the two?

* * *

"I got here as soon as I could. The phone has been ringing off the wall at City Hall. Reporters from all over have been calling about Ivan's murder. Would you believe, even the big Albany television stations have called." Candie tossed her purple wool scarf on the chair next to her coat. True to her word, she'd showed up to help me with my signing today.

"Why would the news people be calling City Hall? Wouldn't they get their information from the police station?" I figured that was the usual route they took.

Candie lowered her voice and leaned closer to me. "I know you are aware the station commander's niece is involved in the investigation, but the general public doesn't, so the police are more tight-lipped than ever about what they are releasing to news outlets. I guess they figure their next best hope of getting any snippets of information is the mayor's office."

I smiled at my cousin. "And they figured wrong?"

She ran her slim fingers through her curls. "Yep. Now, let's get this rodeo started. What would you like me to do?"

I glanced around the small room. Child-sized chairs were arranged in a semi-circle around my larger chair. A wooden table sat against the wall, waiting for copies of my book. I pointed to the canvas bag bulging with my books. "How about you spread my books out on the table, and you can manage the sales? After I have the reading, the parents can purchase a book for their child. Once they have bought the book, you send them over to me, and I'll sign it for the child. How does that sound?"

"Sounds like a plan. I'll spread the books out right now." Candie hefted the heavy bag and strode over to the table.

I looked down at Porkchop. He gazed up at me with his warm brown eyes. "Are you ready for your big day?" He cocked his head and wagged his tail. "Okay, the kids will be here any minute, so let's put your costume on." I grabbed the plastic bag containing the costume I'd had made for him by one of Sylvia's dressmakers. Sylvia Hansen owned the local bridal salon, but her dressmaker, Violet Moon, was more than willing to accommodate me. It was a simple costume and probably didn't take more than an hour for her to whip up.

"Hi, Sam."

I turned to see Susan Mayfield clutching the hands of her adorable children, Robby and Molly. Porkchop waddled over and licked the snow off the tips of Susan's boots.

Molly, the older of the two, giggled. "Momma, look at the doggie. You said his name was Porkchop. He looks more like a hot dog to me."

Susan and I both laughed. "Out of the mouths of babes," I said.

Robby stood silently next to his mother, sucking his thumb.

"If you only knew what they say. Sometimes I think a little old lady has taken over my daughter's body. Any special place we should sit?"

I pointed to the semi-circle of chairs. "You're the first, so you have the pick of chairs. Porkchop and I will be sitting over here." I nodded to the adult-sized chair in front of the children's chairs.

"Momma, I want to sit next to Porkchop," Molly said.

I looked down at Porkchop. "I believe you have a fan, Porkchop."

"Oh, my, yes, coming here today is all Robby and Molly have talked about this week. In fact, she had me up at six this morning, asking when we'd be leaving to come see Porkchop. It's been a long day trying to keep their excitement contained. I'll be dragging at the restaurant tonight."

I laughed. I frankly didn't know where Susan got the energy to raise two young children and help run her and Brian's restaurant. "I don't know how you do it, Susan. It's all I can do to keep up with Porkchop."

Both of us laughed. Susan helped Robby and Molly shed their coats and hats. A riot of red curls sprang out of Robby's hat when Susan lifted it off his head. He looked just like his father, right down to the freckles dotting his small nose. Molly though was the spitting image of her mother. Her long blonde hair was pulled back into a ponytail. Unicorn barrettes were clipped to the sides of her head. Susan placed her children's winter gear over the backs of their chairs.

"Susan, Porkchop and I'll be back in a moment. I have to get the 'star' ready," I said, nodding to Porkchop.

"Okay. I see Candie is manning the book table, so I'll go over and nab the two books I promised for the kids. Right, gang?" Susan said, looking at Robby and Molly, who sat on the floor petting Porkchop.

My pup was in heaven, eating up all the attention.

"Come on, Porkchop. It's almost showtime." I patted my leg for him to follow me.

Jane lent me the use of her office for Porkchop's wardrobe change.

* * *

I pulled a small mirror out of my purse and held it up to Porkchop. "What do you think? Violet did a great job. You look positively handsome."

Violet had fashioned a red satin cape for Porkchop. She'd stitched a P with a lightning bolt shooting through it on the center of the back. He looked just like the superhero he had inspired for my book. I swear he puffed out his chest when he saw his reflection in the mirror.

"Ready?" I asked him as I walked towards the door.

I opened the door to Jane's office. Porkchop strutted before me towards the room designated for our book signing.

"And here they are. The stars of today's story hour, Porkchop and Sam. Can we give them a welcoming round of applause?" Jane Burrows stood before a packed room of preschoolers and their respective parents.

We walked over and stood next to Jane. "Wow, this is quite a crowd," I whispered to her.

She nodded. "I think it's the biggest one we've ever had for a signing and reading. You two are real celebrities."

My face warmed at her compliment. Who knew my little book would be so popular? My eyes took in the faces of the adults and children gathered. They came to rest on one I never expected to see here.

CHAPTER TWENTY-TWO

Sunny Foxx. What was she doing here? And who was the small boy sitting on her lap?

Was this woman stalking me? She couldn't get her claws into my boyfriend, so was she going to sabotage my book signing? Surely, she wouldn't do anything in front of all of these children. I'd have to keep an eye on her so she wouldn't ruin Porkchop's and my big day.

"Oh, look. He really is a super dog. Look at his cape. Just like Superman," said a little girl with long brown pigtails sitting on the floor next to Molly.

Molly turned to the girl and said, "My momma said he can fly."

I groaned inwardly. I hoped the children weren't expecting a display of Porkchop's superpowers. He could eat his kibble faster than a speeding bullet, but fly? Nope.

"Hi everyone. Porkchop, the Wonder Dog, and I want to welcome you today and thank you for coming to see and hear us. I hope you have as much fun listening to Porkchop's story as we had writing it." I scooped Porkchop up in my arms so the children sitting towards the back of the crowd could get a good look at him. Murmurs of "he's so cute" and "I love him" floated up to us. I even heard one child ask his mother if he could have a doggie just like Porkchop. I wondered if he'd get his wish.

The pigtailed girl wriggled on the brightly covered carpet. Her hand shot up in the air.

"Hi," I said. "What's your name?"

The little girl's face beamed with a smile. "Skyla. My name is Skyla, and this is my little brother Micah." Skyla poked a finger at the young boy sitting cross-legged on the floor next to her. Dark-brown curls bounced about his head. His crystal-blue eyes reminded me of Hank's. I wondered if Hank had ever been fortunate enough to have a boy if he'd look like this little fellow sitting in front of me.

"My brother still sucks his thumb at night when he's sleeping," Skyla said, as if she was divulging a deep dark family secret.

Micah glared at his sister. "I do not," he said, jutting out his small chin.

Laughter erupted from the parents and grandparents in the room. Skyla's mother shook her head and leaned over her children. She told them to behave.

I settled Porkchop at my feet and picked up my book someone had placed on my chair. Jane most likely.

"Okay, are you all ready to hear Porkchop's story?"

The young children sitting on the floor staring up at me, along with those sitting on the small chairs, all clapped and nodded for me to begin.

"Once upon a time in the small town of Wings Falls, a puppy was born, but not just any ordinary puppy. This puppy would grow up and become a superhero…"

"Momma, that's where we live. Do you think Spot is a superhero, too?" asked a little girl with curly brown hair like mine.

A smile spread across my face. My heart melted at the thought my book had sparked this child's imagination.

Half an hour later, after many questions from the children, I closed the book and placed it on the small table Jane had set up next to me. I opened the bottle of water she had also provided and took a swallow.

My sweet pup had been content to lay at my feet while I read his story. Occasionally, he lifted his head when a child asked a question.

"Can I pet Porkchop?" Susan's daughter, Molly, asked.

I raised an eyebrow at Susan. "If your mommy says it's okay."

"Please, please, Mommy." Molly looked up at her mother with pleading eyes.

Susan glanced at me. "I guess so, but you have to be very gentle."

This set off a roomful of requests from the other children.

"How about we all get in a line, and one-by-one you can all come up and pet him? I know he'd love it." I didn't know if

Porkchop's ego would ever be the same after today. Would he demand a fluffier bed? A pair of rhinestone-studded sunglasses? Maybe rawhide bones served on a silver platter? Oh, my, what had I done?

Like I'd thought, he preened as each child took their turn lavishing him with pats and attention.

The last child in line was the little boy with Sunny Foxx. He was adorable. I guessed he was about four years old and as cute as could be with a lock of blond hair falling over his forehead. He acted extremely shy. He clung to his mother's leg as they approached Porkchop and me. He wore a faded Superman T-shirt and a pair of jeans that had seen many washings. I hadn't seen Sunny since I discovered her sobbing in Hank's arms.

"Hello, Sunny. I'm surprised to see you here today." Try as I might, I couldn't keep the chill edge out of my voice. After all, this woman wanted to put her claws into my man.

"My uncle mentioned there was going to be an event for children at the library today. He thought Carter, here, would enjoy it." She looked down at the little fellow clinging to her leg. "I didn't know it was going to be you."

"Carter? That's the station commander's first name, too."

Sunny must have realized what I'd thought, because she nodded. "Yes. He's named after my uncle. Uncle Carter and I are very close. In fact, while I was growing up, I spent more time at his house than I did my own. He's been very good to me, especially with all I've been going through. If it wasn't for him, I don't know what little Carter and I would have done. He's been our savior. Can Carter pet Porkchop?"

"Umm, yeah, sure." I was lost in her last statement. What was going on in her life that she needed her uncle's protection?

Sunny led Carter by the hand to Porkchop. "Go on, sweetie. You can pet the doggie."

"He's very gentle and loves little boys like you," I said, trying to give Carter some encouragement. I knew children could be shy, but Carter acted shyer than most children his age.

Carter leaned down and held out a tentative hand to Porkchop. Porkie leaned into the small hand and let the little boy stroke his head. Then my pup licked Carter's hand.

Carter giggled. "Mommy, he licked my hand and it tickled."

"That's his way of giving you a kiss," I said. My heart melted at the smile on his face.

Carter tugged at the leg of Sunny's slacks. "The lady says he kissed me. Mommy, can we get a doggie just like Porkchop?"

"Someday. Someday, Carter, I promise you'll have everything your heart desires."

Carter's face fell. "That's what you always say, Mommy."

"It's time we go now. I need to get to work." Sunny tugged on her son's hand.

"But, Mommy, we didn't get one of Porkchop's books. Please can I have one?" Tears started to trickle down his small cheeks.

"Not today. Maybe when I get paid," Sunny said.

My heart broke watching Carter plead with his mother for one of my books. I picked up the book I had read the children from the small table next to me. "Carter, you know this book I read to everyone?"

He nodded his small head.

"Well, I can't sell it because it's in what I would call 'used condition.' I'd have to throw it away."

Carter gazed at me with his big hazel eyes. "What is 'used fundition'?"

"It means I've already read the book, and I don't think anyone would want a book someone else has read. Do you know of anyone who would like it?"

Carter's eyes grew as big as saucers. He wiggled in his scuffed boots. "I would. I would."

"Can I write your name in the book, Carter?" I asked, reaching for the pen I had placed on the table next to me for that purpose.

Carter clasped his hands in front of him. "Really?"

"Really," I said. "How does 'For Carter, one of Porkchop's biggest fans' sound?"

Carter nodded his head in excitement as I wrote the message in the front of the book.

I closed the book then handed it to Carter. "Here you go. Thank you for coming to visit Porkchop and me today."

Sunny reached out a hand to me. "Thank you," she whispered.

"I hope your son enjoys my book."

Sunny laughed. "I doubt I'll be able to pry it out of his hands. He'll probably sleep with it."

Her words warmed my heart. Could she really be involved with Ivan's murder? Why did she find it necessary to hang all over Ivan at the Fireman's Ball? Was she desperate for a man, any man? Finally, who was Carter's father, and where was he?

CHAPTER TWENTY-THREE

Now that all the children had petted Porkchop, Jane stepped forward. "Thank you all for attending the reading of *Porkchop, the Wonder Dog.* You can purchase a copy over there at that table." She pointed to the table where Candie sat, ready to handle the book sales. My cousin waved her bejeweled fingers at the adults and children.

"After you purchase your book, you can come back over to Sam, and she'd be happy to sign it for you," Jane said.

I smiled and held up my pen. I was thrilled to see all who attended my signing were in line to purchase a copy of my book. This made my writing heart sing.

* * *

Candie handed me the few unsold books from the table. I placed them in the canvas bag I had used to bring them to the library.

"Luckily, I'm going home with a much lighter load than when I came in today," I said.

"Sweetie, you and Porkchop were a huge success. You need to get busy on a sequel to this book." Candie handed me the envelope she'd placed my sales money in.

"I'm working on it. Speaking of a success… How is your latest romance novel coming?" Candie's streamy romance novels were doing rather well. Her newest book, *Hot Night in Paradise*, was climbing the Amazon charts.

"It's doing pretty good. We'll see how it goes."

I was surprised at her dejected tone of voice.

"Will you have any book signings for it? I know your audience is completely different than mine, but maybe you could have one here at the library. I'd be glad to help."

Candie laughed. "I don't think there would be anyone from today attending. Can you imagine the stories little Mary or Johnnie would bring to the playground? I'd be arrested."

I joined in her laughter. "I can see the headline in the *Tribune* right now." With my hands, I framed an imaginary newspaper headline. "Mayor's wife arrested for corrupting children's minds."

"Yeah, not a good look for Mark or me."

Jane walked over to us. "Sam, your reading and signing was a great success. Thank you for coming."

"Thank you for having us. Porkchop, it's time to head home." My pup, who had been lying quietly at my feet, raised his head at the sound of his name.

"Umm, Jane, I didn't mean to intrude on your phone conversation earlier with Jim. Is everything all right with the two of you?" I hoped everything was fine with them. It wasn't easy finding love later in life, not that I thought being in our midfifties was over the hill.

Jane began to fidget with the neck of her sweater. "We're fine. Things have been a little crazy since Ivan's death is all."

"I bet hosting the Firemen's Convention took up a lot of his time, too. It probably cut into a lot of your time together."

Jane nodded, then glanced at her watch. "I need to get home. Jim is coming over for dinner. If you need anything, Penny Richards can help you. She's a very dependable person."

I blinked. Jane certainly was in a hurry to end our conversation. "Yes, she is. I've known her since she was a youngster. Thank you for letting me read my book today. I really appreciate it. Guess I'll see you next Monday at Loopy Ladies."

"Sure, sure. No problem. I'll see you then." Jane waved at us over her shoulder and scurried out of the room.

"What was that all about?" Candie asked, her eyebrows raised in question.

I shook my head. "Darned if I know. Did you notice the other night at the ball when Ivan came up to our table, he made a cryptic remark to Jim having to do with firecrackers? What do you think that was all about? He also mentioned his brother. What did it have to do with Jim?"

"I couldn't begin to guess. I thought he was referring to summer, when a lot of the local towns put on weekly firework displays for the tourists who flood the area. Do you think he could have been referring to something else?"

I placed the last book in my bag. "There's one way to find out."

"How?" Candie asked, gathering up her purse.

I snapped Porkchop's leash on his collar then hitched my brown leather Fendi purse up my shoulder. "Follow me." Porkchop trotted next to me as we left the room.

"Everything all right, ladies?" Penny Richards met us as we exited the room. She bent and scratched Porkchop between the ears.

"Hi. Yes, everything went smoothly. It was a huge success. Jane said she needed to get home. Hopefully, you'll find the room as neat as when I came this morning," I said, anxious to get to my destination.

"Oh, Sam, I know we don't have to worry about you. But you can't believe some of the groups we have here. Why, you'd think a tornado had touched down in the library by the time they left."

Porkchop began to whine. He'd been the perfect puppy this afternoon, and I knew his patience with me was wearing thin. "Sorry, Penny, but I need to get Porkchop home. It's time for his dinner, and I think I hear his tummy rumbling."

"I'm sorry, Porkchop." Penny reached down and ran a hand down his back. She straightened and looked at me. "Thank you again for coming today. I know the kids, parents, and grandparents had a great time."

"We had a ball, too," I said and waved goodbye.

"Where are we going?" Candie asked as we stepped into the library's elevator. I punched the button for the first floor.

"The computer room. I want to do a little research on Jim Turner. Did you notice how evasive Jane was when I mentioned Jim?"

Candie leaned against the stainless-steel wall of the elevator. "Now that you mention it, a clam has looser lips than she does. She wasn't about to spill any beans about her love. Had to get home to fix dinner. Does she think we all just fell off the cotton truck?"

I laughed at my cousin's choice of words. It's probably why her novels are so popular. "Yes, she does."

The elevator binged, and the steel doors slid open. We'd arrived on the first floor. My fingers itched to type in Jim's name and see what we could discover. I waved to a few people I knew as we walked the short distance to the computer room. When we reached the room, I pushed open the door. Long tables ran down both sides of the room, on which sat fifteen computers for public use. Three of them were occupied, two by teenagers who I assumed were doing research for a school project—on second thought, by their giggles, I wondered if their research had more to do with the current teen heartthrob. At the third sat an older woman with gray hair cut in a bob that skimmed her shoulders. As I walked by her, I noticed she was reading an article on cruises in the Caribbean. A great topic, I thought, for dreary March in upstate New York.

I set my bag of books on the floor and pulled out a chair in front of a computer far enough away from all of them so they couldn't see what Candie and I were going to research. I wanted what we discovered to be between the two of us. Jim Turner was well known around town, and I didn't want the gossip mill to start up.

The library had access to files the average person didn't on their home computer.

"What are we looking for?" Candie asked, pulling up a chair next to me.

Porkchop had settled at my feet. Poor pup. I really needed to stop by the butcher shop, Meat of the Matter, and buy him a special dog bone for his long day at the library. He was behaving so patiently.

I clicked on the computer and entered my library password. "I really don't know, but Jane has been acting so secretive about Jim. Did you notice how she suddenly needed to get home to prepare him dinner? I wonder if he's hiding something that could relate to Ivan's murder."

Candie placed her coat over the back of her chair. "I overheard her say that, but maybe she really did have to get home and make dinner for her main squeeze."

I glanced over at her and did an eye roll.

I typed in Jim's name, and pages of articles appeared on the screen. I should have suspected as much, with him being the town's fire chief. "How are we going to narrow the search? We can't possibly read all these." I tapped on the computer's screen.

Candie pointed a finger at the keyboard. "Type in Ivan's name and the word *fireworks*."

I did as my cousin suggested. "Oh, my, what do you make of this?"

CHAPTER TWENTY-FOUR

———

Teen loses fingers and eye in fireworks accident appeared on the screen before us. "Do you think Jim was involved in this accident?" Candie asked, squinting at the screen. She really needed to get her eyes examined, sooner rather than later.

"Let me read it. Maybe this has to do with Ivan's jab at Jim on Saturday night." I scrolled down the screen. The article was dated almost forty years ago. Apparently, five boys, like many youngsters, had had a secret hideout in the local woods. They had built a bonfire and were playing a dangerous version of hot potato. According to one of the boys interviewed, they had tied a bundle of sparklers together and were tossing it to one another. The object of the game was to hold on to the sparklers until the very last moment and then toss it into the fire. Unfortunately, the game backfired when the sparklers exploded before they were tossed into the fire. The explosion resulted in one of the boys losing the fingers on his right hand and his left eye. A young volunteer fireman, who responded to the incident, Ivan Kline, gave a statement. "It was a needless accident, and the boy who instigated the foolish game should be held accountable."

Candie sat back in her chair and stared at the screen. "So, Ivan was a volunteer fireman back then. He had to have been very young."

I nodded. "Yes, but teens can join a fire company as a volunteer. Many go on to make it a life-long career. Say Ivan was in his teens. It would make him the right age for what he is today, which I imagine is in his mid to late fifties."

I gazed at the computer screen again. "It doesn't mention the names of the boys involved. They must have all been under eighteen."

Candie waved her bejeweled fingers towards the computer screen. "Since Ivan was throwing his jab at Jim the other night, do you think he was involved in this game gone wrong?"

Porkchop stirred. He was getting restless. It had been a long day for him. "It makes sense. Oh, oh. What if the boy who was injured was the brother Ivan mentioned on Saturday night? He'd have more of a reason to make life miserable for Jim."

Candie bounced in her seat. "Jim was in charge of this past weekend's activities. Could he have had enough of Ivan and, at some point, followed him then committed the murder?"

Candie's theory made sense to me. "How could this accident have been kept quiet all these years? These are small towns we live in."

"Even small towns have their deep dark secrets. Probably, the people back then closed ranks around the boys to protect their futures. Who knows. Maybe there was a settlement that stated Ivan and his family couldn't talk about the incident?"

I nodded. "That makes sense. Ivan's family would have to keep their mouths shut or forfeit their money. Ivan isn't from Wings Falls, so it might have been easier to do. But why would Ivan needle Jim now after all these years?"

Candie tapped a finger against the side of her head. "Hmmm. Interesting question." She sat up straighter in her chair. "I know. What if there was a statute of limitations for the court order and it's up?"

My eyes widened at this scenario. "Yes. And Ivan never forgave Jim, and now, after all these years, he planned to make Jim's life miserable?"

"Brilliant," Candie exclaimed. The heads of the older woman and the teenagers swiveled towards us.

"Sorry," I said.

I leaned towards Candie and whispered, "What if Saturday night was the last straw for Jim and he snapped?"

My shoulders slumped at the thought of Jim being a murderer. "I hate to admit it, but even the nicest person, if pushed too hard, could react in a negative way. Maybe he reached his breaking point."

Porkchop started to whine under the table.

"Okay, sweetie, it's time to go home and feed you some kibble." I shut down the computer and started to gather up my coat and bag of books.

Candie reached for her coat and purse. "Do you really think Jim Turner may have killed Ivan?"

"I don't want to believe it, but it is a possibility."

Candie shook her head. "No way. I can't believe it. Are you going to tell Hank about what we learned?"

I grimaced at the thought of telling Hank what we had discovered on the computer. He wouldn't be happy about what he had referred to as my "poking my pretty little nose" in police business. I couldn't help it if my curiosity got the best of me at times. Okay, most of the time.

"I'll see if he wants to stop over on his way home from work. Maybe I'll tell him then what we've learned."

Candie held the main library door open for Porkchop and me. I shivered as the cold air hit me. The sky was starting to darken. I couldn't wait for the approach of spring and longer daylight hours.

Porkchop strained on his leash. "Hold on, Porkie. We'll be home in a few minutes." Luckily, I lived nearby, and I'd be able to satisfy his and my hunger pangs.

As we approached the library's parking lot, my eyes were drawn to a couple arguing off to my left, three cars down from where Candie and I were parked. They stood next to a rusted and dented older-model truck. The woman had her back to us, but I suspected I knew who she was—Sunny Foxx.

"Alex, leave us alone. I don't want to take a restraining order out against you, but I will if I have to. You know why Carter and I left. Your drugs. We can't take it anymore. This is no way for Carter and me to live. Those so-called friends you invite over are junkies, and I don't want our son to be around them." Sunny's voice sounded desperate.

"Sunny, we were good together. I promise I'll get my act together. Just give me another chance. I need you and Carter."

Candie turned to me and whispered, "It sounds like Sunny is trying to get out of a nasty situation. I may have been engaged eleven times, but none of my exes ever had a drug problem that I had to deal with. I guess I was lucky. Do you think we should step in and see if Sunny needs our help?"

I shrugged my shoulders. "I don't know. This may be something Sunny doesn't want us to know about. Carter is four years old. Unfortunately, I think she's been handling it for a number of years now."

Just as I referred to the little boy, I heard him cry out, "Daddy, don't hurt Mommy. Please don't hit her."

Porkchop tore his leash from my hand and dashed over to the couple.

"Ouch. Where did this mutt come from? Get him off of me."

Candie and I raced over to Sunny and Carter. If the situation wasn't so dire, I'd laugh out loud. Porkchop had the fellow's cuff of his jeans in his teeth. The man—Sunny had referred to him as Alex—was tugging on them with all of his might. I noticed blood dripping on the fellow's worn sneakers.

I bent and grabbed Porkchop's leash. "Porkchop, come on now. That's enough. Let the nasty man go." True, I was prejudging this Alex, but if he had hit Sunny, I'd gladly let Porkchop gnaw on him for a bit longer.

CHAPTER TWENTY-FIVE

———

Carter clung to his mother's leg. Sobs racked his small body. Sunny rubbed a red spot on the side of her face, where I assumed Alex had hit her moments before. She swiped at the tears streaming down her cheeks.

"Is that mutt yours?" Alex pointed an accusing finger at Porkchop.

I jutted out my chin. "Yes, he is, and he's not a mutt. He's a purebred dachshund."

Alex bent to inspect the ankle Porkchop had attacked. "I don't care if he's a purebred skunk. He injured me, and I'm going to sue you."

Porkchop pulled on his leash. I could tell he wanted to finish the job he had started on Alex's ankle.

Candie, who had remained uncharacteristically quiet until now, pushed herself between Alex and me. "Listen, buddy," she said, poking him in the chest. "You hit that woman there." Candie flicked her fingers toward Sunny. "And caused this young'un great distress. If anyone is going to sue, I'd say it's her. My cousin here…" She nodded towards me. "Her boyfriend is a policeman with the Wings Falls Police Department, and my husband just so happens to be the mayor of this sweet town, and we don't cotton to mangy polecats like you."

Alex's face turned white when Candie mentioned who our significant others were. "Umm," Alex stuttered then looked over Candie's shoulder at Sunny. "I'll be in touch latter. You owe me. Don't think you can leave me this easily. We had a good thing going, and I want my son back." With that, he walked around his truck and climbed in.

We stepped away from the truck. It backfired as he tore out of the library parking lot, his tires squealing on the pavement.

"I'm sorry. You don't need to be involved in my messy business." Sunny wrapped her arms around Carter, who gulped in sniffles while clinging to her side.

Candie and I both turned to Sunny. A clear outline of fingerprints showed on her cheek where Alex had hit her. My heart broke for both her and Carter. I wondered if he'd seen Alex hit his mother before and, if so, how many times. No child should have to witness this kind of behavior, let alone should a woman have to put up with it.

"Who is he?"

Sunny looked at me with watery eyes. "Hopefully, my soon-to-be ex."

I kept silent, hoping she would elaborate on her statement.

She apparently wanted to talk. "Alex and I got married after I discovered I was pregnant with Carter. Unfortunately, he started to hang with a really bad crowd and started taking drugs. He blamed everyone but himself that he couldn't get a job and how his life was a mess."

"Why didn't you leave him before this?" my feisty cousin asked.

Sunny stood straighter. "You don't think I haven't tried? Alex is very possessive. Unfortunately, I used to think it was his way of showing me he loved me, but now I know it's a sickness. He's always tracked me down before when Carter and I left him. This time, though, I made up my mind that for the sake of my son and myself, I had to do it. Make the break. Luckily, my uncle Carter offered me a job while his secretary is out on maternity leave. I used to be a school secretary and a darn good one if I say so myself."

While I thought hers was a good attitude to have, why was she coming on to Hank Saturday afternoon when we were there to help set up for the ball, and then that night, she was hanging all over Ivan Kline? Did she really believe what she said, or was it only bravado on her part and she was desperate for a man to take care of her and her son? Did something happen at the ball between her and Ivan that she killed him? Maybe not on purpose. But accidentally? He could have gotten fresh with her, and she left him out in the cold in his drunken condition to die.

"Come on, Carter. Let's get you home and out of this cold. Mommy will make you some chocolate milk when we get there."

"Are you all right to drive home?" I asked. Her encounter with her soon-to-be ex had rattled me, so I felt sure she'd be shaken up, too.

"I'll be fine. I'm staying with Uncle Carter until I can find an apartment, so I'll be safe."

"I wouldn't think the snake would bother you while you're staying with the station commander. It'd be a one-way ticket to the pokey," Candie said.

I agreed with her, but some people had no common sense, and Alex seemed to fit in that category. "Okay, if you're sure. Porkchop is overdue for his kibble, so I want to get him home." At the mention of his favorite food, Porkie's head snapped up. I bent and scratched him between the ears. "Yes, sweetie, you really are a Wonder Dog. You saved the day today."

As Carter and Sunny walked towards their car, I overheard him saying, "Mommy, I know a Wonder Dog, don't I?"

"Yes, you do. He came to our rescue," Sunny said, opening the door to her car. Carter climbed into his car seat. After she buckled her son in, Sunny turned to us and waved. "Thank you again, " she called to Candie and me.

With Porkchop trotting next to me. Candie and I walked towards our cars. "So, what do you think? Did she murder Ivan Kline?" I asked.

She shrugged her shoulders. "Possibly. She apparently has taken a lot of abuse from her husband and left him because of it. Maybe Ivan got fresh with her, and she wasn't about to let him get away with it."

"My thoughts exactly, but we also have Jim Turner to consider and his motive for killing Ivan." We had reached our cars, I opened the door to the Bug and Porkchop hopped onto the passenger seat. Once he was settled, I walked around to the back and popped the trunk and shoved the canvas bag with my unsold books inside. At least it was a lot lighter than when I left home.

"Are you going straight home?" Candie asked from behind me.

"Yes, Porkchop needs his dinner, and I want to settle on the sofa with a glass of wine and hope Hank comes over or at least calls. What about you?"

Candie smiled. "I'm hoping for a romantic night with Mark after he spends some time trying to win Dixie over to his side."

"How is it going?" I hoped the hints for winning a cat's affection we'd thought of were working.

"The catnip and new toys Mark showered her with have made Dixie a little more affectionate towards him, but I think there's a ways to go yet. My cat unfortunately has a long memory and is still fearful Mark will take Annie away, but we are making some progress."

"Progress is a good thing, and I'm happy to hear it. Have a wonderful evening." I hugged her and walked around to the driver's side of the Bug.

"My fingers are crossed you have a great evening with Hank, too," Candie said, opening Precious's driver's-side door.

"Me, too, but you know how it is when he's involved with a murder investigation."

Candie nodded. "Yes, long hours and little time left for romance."

I pulled out of my parking spot, waved at Candie, and tooted the Bug's horn.

She beeped back at me and returned my wave.

* * *

"Porkchop, we had a very successful day at the library. Don't you think?" He lay on the floor next to the sofa, chewing on a rawhide bone. He looked up at me with his chocolate-brown eyes at the mention of his name. He dropped his bone and jumped at the side of the sofa. I shifted my rug hooking farther down the sofa then reached down and pulled him up onto my lap. The crow on a watermelon I was hooking for summer could wait. I needed the comfort my dog offered more right now. The phone hadn't rung since I came home. True, there was a text from Hank stating he'd be working late, but that was all I'd heard from him.

I nuzzled Porkchop's head next to mine. "It's just you and me again tonight."

Porkchop started to squirm in my arms. He jumped off the sofa and ran to the front door. This usually meant only one thing. Hank was here. My heart accelerated at the thought of seeing him. I pushed off the sofa and hurried to the door. Porkchop beat me there. He stood wagging his whole body in excitement.

"Hank," I barely breathed out as I opened the door.

He gazed at me with his crystal-blue eyes. They were clouded with worry.

CHAPTER TWENTY-SIX

"Hank what's the matter? Has something happened?" With his hand grasped in mine, I led him over to the sofa. Porkchop followed, yipping for attention.

Once in the living room, he shed his down coat and tossed it on the wing chair next to the fireplace. He raked a hand through his wavy dark-brown hair, causing the curl to fall on his forehead.

He turned to me and ran a finger down my cheek then pulled me into his arms. He bent his head and placed a kiss on my lips.

"Hank, please tell me what's wrong." Fear snaked through my body. Something was wrong—terribly wrong. I could feel it right down to my toes encased in my fuzzy moose slippers.

"Could I have a beer first? It was rough today at the station."

"Sure. Settle on the sofa, and I'll be right back with a Trail's Head." My refrigerator was always stocked with a few of his favorite beers.

On the way out of my kitchen, I snagged the plastic container off the kitchen counter containing pretzels. It wasn't much, but I didn't think Hank had eaten dinner yet. I'd throw a pizza in the oven when he was up to it. A smile crossed my lips when I walked into the living room. Porkchop was snuggled on Hank's lap. Porkchop lay back with his eyes closed and tail wagging. Hank was giving my pup belly rubs.

I held out the beer to Hank and placed the pretzel container on the wooden trunk in front of the sofa. His strong fingers wrapped around the beer.

"Care for a pretzel?"

He shook his head.

I couldn't wait any longer. I needed to know what was troubling him. "Hank, what's the matter? I'm going to assume it has to do with Ivan's murder. Am I right?"

He nodded but didn't look me in the eyes.

"Hank, please. You're scaring me. Tell me what's wrong."

"I've been taken off the case until further notice."

My mouth dropped open. Hank, off an important case? He was Wings Falls Police Department's lead detective. They'd lured him away from Albany PD because he was so good.

I blinked then blinked again in disbelief at what he had said. If you'd told me it was sunny and ninety degrees outside, I would have found that more believable.

"What? Why?" I stammered.

He reached for my hand and gently squeezed it. With sorrowful eyes, he looked at me. "Because you are now a suspect in Ivan's murder, and so is my aunt Gladys."

I shook my head. "Hank, this is a joke, right? But you're a month early. April Fool's isn't until next month."

Hank placed Porkchop on the floor and gathered me into his arms. "I wish it were a joke. Do you remember the water bottles that were scattered on the ground near the Loopy Ladies' outhouse?"

I nodded against his chest as he stroked my long, curly brown hair. "Yes, I wondered about them because it's unusual to see such trash lying around, but what does that have to do with me?"

"They have your fingerprints on them."

"Wait. That has to be a big mistake. I didn't have any water at the ball on Saturday night. They couldn't possibly be mine."

Was this a sick joke? If so, I wasn't laughing, and it didn't look like Hank was either. Sure, my fingerprints were in the system. Unfortunately, this wasn't the first time I'd been involved in a murder. That was how Hank and I first met over a year ago when I discovered my first dead body. Jeez, this was becoming a nasty—or, should I say, deadly—habit of mine.

I pulled out of Hank's arms and sat back on the sofa cushion. "Wait. Remember Saturday at the center, Martha asked you to fetch her a case of water? I went downstairs with you. A half dozen bottles fell on the floor, and I placed them next to the wall. Of course they'd have my fingerprints on them. Were they used to douse Ivan?"

Hank sat up straighter. "You're right. It'd slipped my mind you did that. I'll make sure Joe knows it."

I pounded the cushion between Hank and me with my fists. "Joe? You mean Joe Peters is now in charge of the investigation? I'm doomed. He's wanted to get back at me since kindergarten when I ratted him out to the teacher for peeing in the sandbox. He'll lock me up and throw away the key. Besides, I didn't even know Ivan Kline until this past weekend. What motive would I have for murdering him?"

Hank reached over and gathered my fists in his hands. He raised them to his lips and placed a kiss on them. "I may be off the case, but I won't let anything happen to you or Aunt Gladys. Even if it costs me my job."

"You said Gladys is a suspect, too. What possible reason would she have in killing Ivan? Like me, did she even know him?"

Hank nodded. "Do you remember when Doc Cordone mentioned Ivan had a bump on his head?"

"Yeah, maybe he slipped on the ice before settling down for a long winter's nap in the outhouse."

A chuckle escaped Hank's lips. "That's one way of putting it, but from what I've learned of Ivan Kline so far, he was no Saint Nick."

"No, from what Candie and I discovered at the library today, he was more like the Grinch who stole Christmas."

Hank raised one of his well-shaped eyebrows at me.

"Don't go looking at me like that. I noticed Ivan wasn't the most well-liked person this past weekend. I saw him arguing with more than one person at the center. You know I had a book reading and signing at the library today."

Hank did a palm-plant on his forehead. "Geez, I'm sorry. I forgot all about that. I've been so wrapped up in this investigation—well, that is until I was kicked off the case because of my relationship with you and Aunt Gladys. How did it go?"

"Fine. No, it was better than fine. It was a huge success, and Porkchop was a big hit. Anyway, to get back to what I was talking about. When I got there, I overheard Jane Burrows on the phone with Jim Turner, and it sounded like they were talking about Ivan. When I asked her about Jim, she got very agitated and wouldn't talk about him. After my signing, Candie and I googled Ivan on the internet and found some very interesting information about him and possibly Jim and a person who we think might be Ivan's brother."

Hank straightened up. "Really? From what I know of Jim, he seems like a pretty straight as an arrow kind of guy. He certainly helps out the police when we need him and his guys. I've heard nothing but good things about him since I moved here."

"I have to agree with you, but in his youth, he may have done something that involved Ivan's brother."

Hank's eyes widened. "Really? Like what?"

I related to him Candie's and my internet findings.

"Wow, that is pretty devastating, but to hold a grudge all these years? I don't know." Hank leaned over and tapped the tip of my nose. "Remember what I've told you in the past about sticking that pretty little nose in other people's business."

I pulled back and jutted out my chin. "If it wasn't for my inquiring mind, Joe Peters would have locked me up long ago."

Hank nodded. "True, but I don't want anything to happen to you."

"You mentioned Gladys is a suspect, too. What could she possibly have to do with Ivan's murder? That's ridiculous. Joe has really lost it if he thinks Gladys killed Ivan."

"I agree with you, but a skillet was found not far from the outhouse, and it had her fingerprints on the handle. A smear of blood was on the bottom of it. It's at the lab right now to determine if the blood is Ivan's."

My lips formed an *O*. I remembered the skillet toss and Gladys taking off her gloves to get a better grip on the skillet's handle.

CHAPTER TWENTY-SEVEN

———

"Come on, Porkchop. Let's go for a walk. I need to clear my mind after everything Hank told us last night." To think I was a suspect in another murder blew me away. I had tried to call Candie after Hank left, but my call went to her voicemail. I was hoping she and Mark were having a romantic evening, so I didn't bother calling back. At least one member of my family could have sweet dreams. Me? Mine were visions of me donning an orange jumpsuit and banging a tin cup against iron bars. I'd call her on her lunch hour to tell her everything Hank had said. She'd be madder than one of Memaw Parker's wet hens if I didn't.

Hank didn't stay late. He said he needed to get home and see to Nina. I understood. I wouldn't have been the best company anyway. The sun was shining this morning, so instead of letting Porkchop out in my backyard to do his business, I felt a brisk walk would do us both good. I hoped the fresh air would help clear my mind of thoughts of Ivan's murder and my being a suspect. I wondered if I should call my lawyer and apprise him of the situation. Would hiring a lawyer make me look more guilty? Joe Peters would certainly think so. Speaking of the devil in a gray uniform, a black and white skidded to a stop in front of Gladys's house. Behind the wheel sat Sergeant Peters. I was surprised he didn't have the car's lights flashing. A deep growl rumbled up from Porkchop's throat when Joe climbed out of the squad car.

Joe leapt up the weathered wooden steps of Gladys's front porch two at a time. He certainly seemed in a hurry to see her. He knocked on her front door, but I couldn't hear the conversation between the two when Gladys answered. From the look on her face, she wasn't too pleased to see him. Her green curls bobbed as she shook her head back and forth. She finally opened her storm door and allowed him to enter her house.

Porkchop growled again. Only this time, he bared his teeth. "I know, Porkie. I'm not particularly fond of Sandy either," I said, using Joe's childhood nickname. "Do you think he's here to grill Gladys about her fingerprints on the skillet? Let's see what he's up to." I led Porkchop up Gladys's front steps. I could hear her voice through the closed door. She wasn't happy with whatever Joe had to say. I tapped on her door then opened it and poked my head into her house. "Gladys, is everything all right? Can I help?"

"Come in," she shouted from her living room.

I pushed the door farther open and walked into a step back in time. The décor of Gladys's living room hadn't changed in decades. A green shag rug covered the hardwood floors. White cotton doilies, like my grandmother would crochet, lay over the arms of a recliner in the corner of the room. Gladys sat on a gold velvet sofa encased in plastic slip covers. Joe sat across from her on a dark wooden rocker. Fringe hung from the lamps sitting on the end tables. Gladys stood when I entered the room and scurried over to me. Worry creased her wrinkled face.

She clasped my free hand into hers then turned to Joe and pointed an accusing finger. "Sandy, here, wants to arrest me for murder. Can you believe that?"

I cringed when she used Joe's hated childhood nickname. True, I often slipped and used it myself, but I knew he wouldn't take kindly to Gladys for calling him by that name.

Joe looked at me with a smug expression on his face. His unibrow raised when he said, "Good to see you, Ms. Davies. Your being here will save me a trip next door."

"What do you want, Joe?" Although, after my conversation with Hank last night, I had an inkling as to what he wanted. I could almost feel those metal bracelets squeezing my wrists.

"I'm here investigating the murder of Ivan Kline. I have some pertinent questions to ask you and Mrs. O'Malley."

Porkchop tugged on his leash. I needed to keep a firm grip on him, for fear he'd break loose and chomp on Joe's ankle. That's all I'd need to be arrested for, siccing my fierce dog on him. At least Porkie had stopped growling.

I glanced around the room. "Gladys, where is Frank? I think he should be here."

Gladys sniffled. "This morning he went to Bowlerama to bowl with his buddies. I don't want to disturb him for this nonsense." She waved her gnarled fingers at Joe.

I glanced at my watch. It read eight o'clock. Would the bowling alley be open now? "This early in the morning?"

Gladys nodded. "Yes, he and his buddies bowl before the alley opens. The guys get a little rowdy and disturb the other bowlers, so the owner of the lanes lets them come in early to do all the hooting and hollering they want."

I led Gladys back to the sofa. When I sat, air whooshed out of the seats. Porkchop crouched at attention at my feet. I turned to Joe. "Okay, Joe. What is this all about? You mentioned Ivan's death." I played dumb and asked, "What does this have to do with Gladys and me?"

His unibrow crawled up his forehead again. "You mean your boyfriend, Hank, hasn't told you?"

My dander shot up at the way he sneered the word *boyfriend*. I lied, "No, Detective Johnson is way too professional to share information on an active investigation with me."

Joe grunted as if he didn't believe me.

I didn't care whether he did or not. I just wanted him out of Gladys's house.

Joe reached in his jacket and pulled out a small notepad and flipped it open. "Mrs. O'Malley, where were you Saturday night about the hour of ten p.m.?"

Gladys looked at me and blinked, clearly surprised by his question. "Home in bed with Frank. Why do you ask?"

Joe puffed up his chest. I feared the already straining buttons on his shirt would pop. "I'll ask the questions here. Can you prove you were there? Just answer me, please."

Gladys leaned forward on the sofa. She pointed a shaking gnarled finger at Joe. Oh, no. He didn't want to deal with an angry Gladys, and I could tell her temper was rising. "What do you think we do, you fool? Invite people to join us in bed?"

I placed a hand over my mouth and pretended to cough to hide the laughter that wanted to escape. Joe was treading on dangerous ground by getting Gladys mad.

"Are you sure?" Joe persisted.

"Of course I am. What do you think I am? Senile?"

The one thing you couldn't accuse her of was not having all her wits about her. She was sharper than me on some days. I reached over and patted her hand, hoping to calm her down. Getting on Joe's bad side wouldn't help her. I knew that from personal experience.

Joe eyed Gladys again. "Can you explain why your skillet was used to conk Ivan Kline on the head?"

"How do you know it was mine? There were at least six other contestants in the competition."

Joe shifted on his seat. He looked uncomfortable. He must have realized that Gladys was a tough person to interview. "All six skillets have been accounted for, and only one has fingerprints on the handle. They match the ones the state has on file for you."

"Of course I can. I took off my gloves when I threw the dang thing at the skillet toss."

My eyebrows shot up at Joe's statement. "Why would the state have your fingerprints on file?" I knew they had mine, but Gladys? Did she have a criminal past I didn't know about? Hank had never mentioned anything about his aunt being a jailbird. Not that it's something one would brag about. We all have skeletons in our closets.

Gladys waved my question away. "Last year, the Wings Falls Senior Center invited the police in to fingerprint any senior who wished to have it done."

"Why would they do that?" I still wasn't clear about the reason for the fingerprinting.

Gladys looked at me as if I were a dense block of wood. "Because as we age, some of us get forgetful and might wander off from our homes. It's a way of identifying the poor lost soul. Not that Frank or I are in that category."

Joe tapped his pad of paper with a pen to get our attention. "Ladies, can we please get back to my questions. Mrs. O'Malley, I understand you had a past history with the deceased."

My head whipped around to Gladys. This was news to me.

CHAPTER TWENTY-EIGHT

———

Gladys's mouth dropped open even farther than mine, if that was possible. "What are you talking about? What history?"

Joe flipped through his notepad. He stopped turning the pages and looked up at Gladys. "I have it on good authority that you and Ivan's father were once engaged and that he broke it off. Were you the jilted lover and decided to take your revenge out on his son?"

Gladys stood and placed her hands on her slim hips. "Why you little twit. I've known you since you were in diapers, and you have the gall to accuse me of such a thing. If you must know, your source, whomever that may be, is wrong. I was the one to break off the engagement. I decided I was too young to get married, and thank heavens I did, or I would never have found my Stan."

Frank may be the love of Gladys's life now, but Stan was Captain Stan, Gladys's deceased husband, who made his living as a fisherman. I glanced out the side window and spotted his rotting boat in Gladys's backyard, where his ashes resided in an urn placed in front of the steering wheel.

Red crept up Joe's neck as he tugged at the collar of his uniform shirt. He turned to me. Drat. Now he was going to shift his grilling to me.

"Ms. Davies, can you explain why your fingerprints are all over the water bottles found at the crime scene?"

I took a deep breath and reached down to pet Porkchop. He'd kept his eyes on Joe the whole time, as if daring Joe to give him a reason to attack. I straightened in my seat. "Joe, if you corroborated your information with Detective Johnson, you'd know that he and I were helping at the Civic Center Saturday afternoon. We had a request to fetch a case of water bottles for Martha Callaway. About a half dozen bottles fell off the stack of cases when Detective Johnson pulled it down. I didn't want to leave them scattered on the floor, so I picked them up and set the bottles next to the wall. You can double check this statement with the detective."

Joe cleared his throat. "Oh, I will. Believe me, I will."

"Is there anything else you want to know?" I asked.

Joe looked me in the eye. "One last question. Where were you Saturday night after the ball?"

Now it was my turn to blush. "With Detective Johnson. If you don't believe me, you can ask him about that, too. I'm sure you'll agree, he has a sterling reputation, and you can believe what he says about my whereabouts on Saturday night."

Joe flipped his notepad shut and rose from his chair. "That's all for now, ladies, but don't leave town. You may be wanted for further questioning."

A growl rumbled up from Porkchop's throat. I bent and petted his back. "That's okay, sweetie. The man is leaving."

"Idiot," Gladys murmured under her breath.

I had to agree, but I didn't want to say it out loud for fear Joe had heard her and would use it as an excuse to make our lives miserable until the police found Ivan's killer.

"You can let yourself out," Gladys shouted at Joe's back. She shifted on the sofa towards me. "He's always been an unsufferable man. How Hank puts up with him at the station I don't know."

"Hank says he's a good cop, so I guess we have to give him that."

The front door slammed opened. "Gladys, is everything all right? A police car just pulled out of our driveway." Frank, Gladys's live-in love, stepped into the room.

Gladys jumped off the sofa and ran to Frank, flinging her arms around his neck. Frank dropped his bowling bag at his feet and wrapped his arms around her. "Oh, Pookie Bear, it was just awful. The police think I killed Ivan Kline. That officer grilled me until I thought I would faint."

Frank pulled back from Gladys. "That's just nonsense. Why would he think such a thing?"

"He said that my fingerprints are on the skillet used to whack Ivan upside his head. Ohhh, Pookie, I can feel the shackles clamping around my wrists right now. Will you visit me in the Big House? I hope I don't have to become BFFs with Big Bertha, Frank. Orange isn't my best color. I don't have the correct complexion for it. I never imagined spending my final days in prison," Gladys wailed as Frank led her towards the sofa.

I bent and whispered to Porkchop, "Let's leave them alone. I need to call Hank and Candie and tell them about Joe's visit."

Porkchop and I quietly left Frank comforting Gladys on the sofa. I doubted they were aware we had left.

As soon as we entered my house, Porkchop beelined it for the kitchen. He stood next to his bone-shaped food bowl, waiting for me to fill it with his kibble. "Okay, you were so good at Gladys's, you deserve a small helping." I reached into the upper cabinet where it was stored and plinked a handful into the bowl. "I'm happy you didn't take a chunk out of Sergeant Peters' ankle."

While Porkie was devouring his food, I grabbed my phone off the counter and punched in Hank's number. My shoulders slumped as I heard it go to his voicemail. I didn't want to relay this morning's events in a message, so I said I hoped he was having a good day. Next, I hit Candie's number. She picked up on the first ring.

"Hi, sugar. What's up?"

Her southern accent brought a smile to my lips. "I had an interesting morning." I relayed to her what went down at Gladys's house.

"Why that no-good, egg-sucking hound dog. I'll string him up by his toes."

Porkchop glanced up at me from his bowl as I laughed out loud at my cousin's description of Joe. She didn't mince words.

"I'm finished here at noon. Let's meet at Sweetie Pie's for lunch so we can plan our strategy for proving you and Gladys innocent of Ivan's murder."

My shoulders slumped and I groaned. "Not again. Another murder to solve."

"Cheer up, sweetie. When it comes to solving murders, we are batting a thousand."

My cousin was correct. We had been successful, much to Hank's chagrin about my involvement, in solving the past four murders that plagued Wings Falls.

"Okay, I'll meet you at Sweetie Pie's, in our regular booth at a little after noon."

Porkchop finished his kibble and stared up at me. "I know, your buddy Hank isn't going to like it, but what can I do, Porkie? Joe sees Ivan's murder as his big chance to get back at me for ratting him out all those years ago for peeing in the school's sandbox. He thinks my fingerprints on those water bottles nails me for the murder."

* * *

I slid into Candie's and my favorite red vinyl–clad booth and placed my pink Kate Spade purse on the seat. The booth sat next to a window where we could watch people walking down Main Street.

"Okay, let's solve this murder."

I turned away from gazing out the window to see my cousin toss her purse on the bench seat and sit across from me.

Strands of her auburn hair had escaped from the loose bun at the nape of her neck and floated about her face. The cold air outside had given her cheeks a rosy glow. "Now tell me again what Sandy Peters accused you of."

Her use of his dreaded nickname made me smile as I relayed the latest developments.

"Why that lamebrain duck. He thinks you committed murder with that flimsy evidence?"

I nodded. "Yes, and if not me, he wants to pin it on Gladys since her prints were on the skillet used to conk Ivan in the head."

Candie's violet eyes widened. "Who does he think you two are, some murdering duo running rampant in Wings Falls? Well, we'll just prove him wrong. Who else do you think had it in for Ivan?"

I thought of my other suspects and wasn't fond of my choices. The ones I knew all seemed like good people. I found it just as hard to believe they'd kill Ivan as Gladys and myself.

CHAPTER TWENTY-NINE

―――――

"Afternoon, ladies. Do y'all care for a cup of coffee?"

I glanced up to see Franny Goodway grasping two pots of coffee in her dark hands, one regular and the orange-banded one. I smiled at Franny's southern drawl, which was just about as thick as Candie's. Her restaurant had been a local favorite since she flipped over her open sign.

I turned over the mug sitting in front of me. "Sure. I'd love some."

Candie did the same with hers.

We were such regular customers of Franny's that I didn't even have to mention my decaf preference to her. She knew which to serve to each of us.

"Are you here for lunch or just want to gab over a cup of coffee?"

"Honey, I'm starving. That mayor in City Hall works me to death." Candie reached for the menus tucked behind the metal napkin holder at the end of the table. She handed one to me and opened her own.

"BLT sandwiches with a side of sweet potato fries is the special today. I can also include a slice of my banana cream pie for dessert."

"Ooh wee. Franny, you're going to do some serious harm to my waistline, offering such scrumptious meals."

Franny and I laughed. "Franny, I have to agree with Candie, but I can't pass up such a tempting meal, either. I'll have that, and don't forget the banana cream pie for dessert."

Franny placed the coffeepots on our table. She pulled a receipt pad and pencil out of the short black apron tied around her slim waist and jotted down our orders. "Is that all, ladies?" she asked, tucking the pad and pencil back into her apron.

"Yes," Candie and I said in unison.

I laughed. "After we polish off that meal, I'll have to hit the gym double time for a week, but it will be worth it."

Franny grabbed the coffeepots and walked towards the kitchen to place our orders.

Candie leaned across the scarred red Formica tabletop. "Do you still get up at that nasty early hour and go to the gym?"

For a few months, I had gotten into the routine of rising at five in the morning and trudging off to the local gym, but lately I'd let it slide. Snuggling into the covers of my warm bed on these cold winter mornings had been too inviting. "Weeellll, I can't say I've been very faithful about going. I really need to get back into the habit. Especially after I finish the meal Franny will be delivering to us."

I glanced around Sweetie Pie's and took in its homey 50s décor. I loved everything about it, from the black and white checkered pattern tiles of the floor to the waitress's uniforms that featured a lacy handkerchief flowing out of the breast pocket and the tabletop jukeboxes placed at the end of every table. I flipped through the selection of songs. They also were filled with songs from that era. "What would you like to listen to? Roy, Elvis, Dolly?"

Candie rolled her eyes. "I believe we have more important issues to decide, other than what song I'd like to listen to. How about we find out who murdered Ivan before I have to forward your next Christmas card to the state penitentiary?"

I groaned. "If you insist. I was hoping to enjoy my meal before bringing up my future fate."

Candie reached into her purse and pulled out a pad of paper and a pen. She tapped the pad with a ruby red fingernail. "I insist. First, we know you didn't kill Ivan, nor did Gladys. So, let's review the other possible suspects."

I wrinkled up my forehead. "Please... Can't I enjoy my meal first? I really don't want to spoil my delicious BLT sandwich and banana cream pie thinking about murder."

Candie heaved a big sigh. The rhinestones on her blouse twinkled under the lights of the café. If nothing else, I could depend on my cousin to add some sparkle to my life. "All right, but as soon as you swallow your last bite of pie, we're getting down to business and searching for Ivan's killer."

"Okay." I reached for my purse and plucked out my wallet. I dug through it for two quarters, the price of a song from the jukebox.

I flipped through the song selection cards and decided on E-7, Elvis's "Hound Dog." I slipped the coins into the slot, and soon the 50s hip-wriggler was singing to us.

"That's an appropriate song for Peters. Him, trying to accuse you of murder. My Dixie will grow wings before he can prove you did it."

I silently hoped she was correct.

"Here you go, ladies."

I looked up to see Franny next to our table. A huge tray containing out meals rested on her shoulder. Candie and I scooted back in our seats so she could lay the dishes before us. "I don't know how you can balance those trays like you and the rest of the waitstaff do. I'd be a disaster, spilling everything."

Franny finished unloading the tray. "After all these years of owning Sweetie Pie's, it's second nature to me now."

"I bet you get a better workout lifting those trays than I do at the gym."

Franny laughed and flexed a bicep at us. She confirmed what I suspected. Her muscles were better toned than some I'd seen on guys lifting weights at the gym.

"Instead of paying for a gym membership, you should work for Franny," Candie said as she blobbed catsup on the side of her plate for her sweet potato fries.

I shook my head. "No way. At the gym if I dropped a weight, no disaster done. Here, can you imagine if a dropped a tray of food? Oh, my—the mess."

"So, I'll put you on my 'never hire' list," Franny said with a chuckle.

I reached for the catsup bottle from Candie. "If you have such a list, I'd write it down in big letters and highlight it."

A smile crossed Franny's face. "Duly noted. Enjoy your meal. I'd better get back to the kitchen and make sure things are humming there."

* * *

I leaned back against my booth seat and groaned. "Next time I order such a large meal, smack me."

Candie swirled her fork around the plate that moments ago held her banana cream pie. She placed the fork to her lips and licked off the last bit of pie crumbs. She closed her eyes. A look of pure delight crossed her face. "But it was sooo good."

She was right. It was so good.

Candie pushed herself up and reached for her pad and pen. "All right, enough stalling. Now down to business."

I felt my stomach churn. So much for enjoying my meal. Candie was right. I couldn't put off trying to figure out who really killed Ivan any longer. Not if I didn't want to wind up in the Big House with Gladys, becoming BFFs with Big Bertha.

CHAPTER THIRTY

———

"Candie, this is going to be really tough. I know most of the suspects I have in mind and can't imagine any of them as a murderer. I mean, I've known Jim Turner for years."

"What about the dirt we dug up on him at the library? From what we overheard at the ball on Saturday night when Ivan referred to fireworks and his brother, we know that he was harassing Jim."

I shook my head, not wanting to believe Jim was the murderer. People irked other people every day, but they don't murder them for being a jerk, and from what I was learning about Ivan Kline, he was an A-number-one jerk.

"Ivan's brother has to be the teen who lost his fingers and an eye because of the foolishness those boys engaged in years ago. Seeing his brother disabled like that might have been a constant reminder for Ivan." Candie lifted the mug to her lips and took a sip of her coffee.

I drew a circle with my fingertip on the red tabletop, thinking of what Candie had said. "You're right. It might have been something Ivan couldn't brush away lightly. It would be like an open, festering wound that wouldn't go away. But what good would it do now for him to bring it up to Jim? It's been years since the incident."

Candie sat up straight in the booth. "Yes, but Jim is talking about retiring, and there would probably be a ton of accolades for his years of service. Maybe Ivan couldn't bear to hear all the praise the community organizations would heap on Jim."

I jumped in my seat with excitement. "Soooo, he decided to drag up the past and ruin Jim's reputation. It certainly would upset Jim. But do you think enough for him to murder Ivan?"

Candie shrugged. "I don't know, but it is possible. It certainly gives Peters another suspect besides you and Gladys to look at."

"Mommy, can we sit over there by the window? I want to see the trucks as they drive past."

I turned towards the small voice wanting a window seat and was surprised to see Martha Callaway walking in our direction holding a young boy's hand. I leaned over the table and whispered to Candie, "Look, that's Martha Callaway with her son."

"So?" Candie said.

"So, her son has been very ill with cancer. Hank mentioned his station took up a collection to help defray lodging costs when she has to take her son to Boston for treatment."

A frown creased Candie's smooth forehead. "Okay, so what's the big deal? She's going to treat her boy to a meal at Sweetie Pie's."

"Candie, if you need to take donations to help with the costs of your son's cancer treatments, can you afford to eat out? You know, I saw Martha arguing with Ivan Saturday at the Center. Did Ivan have some dirt on Martha that he was hanging over her head?"

Candie waggled her fingers at me in excitement. "Since she is in a bad financial strait, what if he accused her of skimming money off the food sales? Could she have murdered him because of that?"

"Hi, ladies."

I glanced up to see Martha and her son standing at the end of our table. She clutched his small hand. A baseball cap was perched on his head. Most likely to hide the fact that he had lost his hair due to his chemo treatments. Heat crawled up my neck. I hoped she hadn't overhead what Candie and I were discussing. "Umm, hi Martha. Who is this handsome young man?"

The boy squirmed at his mother's side. "This is Jaxson. My mother gave us a gift certificate to Sweetie Pie's, so we're here to celebrate his perfect checkup from his doctor."

A smile spread across Jaxson's face. "Yeah, I don't have to go to that hospital anymore."

I clapped my hands. "That's wonderful. I can recommend everything on the menu. You won't be disappointed."

Martha laughed. "That narrows down our food choices. Jaxson, you ready to find a seat?"

"Yes, Mommy," he said, tugging on her hand.

They turned to walk away.

"Enjoy," I called after them.

Candie tapped the tabletop with her fingernails. "Cute kid, isn't he? I'm sure this has been devastating for Martha. Do you really think she might have done something illegal?"

I spread my fingers out in front of me on top of the table and studied them as if they'd give me the answer to Candie's question. "I don't know. A mother would do anything to protect her child. She was handling a lot of cash this past weekend at the Civic Center at the refreshment area. What if Ivan saw her pocket some of the money? Everyone was so busy with the setup for the ball, and later at the dance with the crowds of people there, who would have noticed if she slipped a few bills into her pocket? Except maybe Ivan."

"Oh, oh." Candie squirmed in her seat. "Yes, and what if he told her he saw her do it and threatened to report her to the police? You know, blackmail."

My brow furrowed. "What could she possibly give him as a payoff? She doesn't have any money. She's not working, and what little she does have is going towards bills for Jaxson's care."

"Oh, come on, Sam. Sex. Martha is a very attractive woman. Ivan not so much. What if he told her he'd forget what he saw if she'd give him a 'little lovin'?"

I tapped the side of my head with a finger and thought over what Candie had said. "Hmmm. That certainly is possible. There were times at the ball when I noticed someone had replaced her at the cash box. I assumed she was taking a potty break or possibly helping out in the kitchen."

Candie nodded her head vigorously. "Yes, yes." Excitement laced her Southern drawl. "I know it's sad to think she'd do such a thing, but I'm sure she's a Momma Bear and would do anything to protect her cub."

I had to agree with my cousin. "One of the times she was missing from the refreshment table, she might have agreed to meet Ivan outside. He could have gotten fresh with her. He was pretty drunk. Maybe she picked up a skillet to defend herself from his unwanted advances, then grabbed a couple of the water bottles to cool down his libido. He was soused enough to pass out in the outhouse and not realize how cold it was outside."

"If all this is true, would Martha be able to waltz back into the Civic Center and calmly resume her cashiering duties? And where was Sunny Foxx all this time? She had been hanging on Ivan's arm earlier."

I shrugged my shoulders. "Heck if I know. After we ate our dinner, Hank and I were too busy on the dance floor to pay attention to what was going on at the buffet line."

Candie smiled. "Yeah, so I noticed."

I laughed and threw my wadded-up paper napkin at her. "I hate to think of Martha as Ivan's murderer, or from what I've learned about Sunny Foxx, her either, but I don't want Peters pinning it on me."

"Okay, so who do we look at now as the prime suspect?" Candie asked, tossing the napkin back at me.

Just then, Drew Ellis walked past the window next to our booth. I glanced back at Candie. "What are you doing tonight? Do you want to go to the Wings Falls firehouse and play a few games of bingo?"

Candie's eyebrows raised. "Bingo? Since when do you fancy a game of bingo?"

"Since I've been accused of murdering Ivan Kline."

CHAPTER THIRTY-ONE

―――――

"Geez, I never knew this was such a popular game," Candie said, as I pulled my Bug into the packed parking lot of the Wings Fall Fire Company banquet hall.

"Me neither. I know a number of the Loopy Ladies come." I nodded towards the flagpole that stood in front of the firehouse. "I see the American flag is flying at half-mast. I wonder if that is in honor of Ivan's death."

Candie turned in her seat and stared out the Bug's passenger window. "Probably. I don't know of any dignitaries who have died lately they would have lowered the flag for."

"Seeing as how Jim Turner and Ivan had a contentious relationship, it is mighty nice of him to recognize Ivan's passing. I figured postponing bingo from Tuesday evening to Wednesday night would have been enough of an honor for Ivan," I said. This was the first time in my memory I'd known of the shifting of the scheduled popular game night. Nothing, and I mean nothing, got in the way of these diehard players. Not wind, rain, or a threatened snowstorm.

I finally found an empty parking space towards the side of the building and slipped the Bug into it.

Candie gathered up her rhinestone-studded purse and reached for the door handle. She stopped and glanced back at me. "If Jim had such a falling out with Ivan, do you think he would have honored him in such a way? Wouldn't he just ignore Ivan's death?"

I thought over what she had said. "I guess he would. Certainly, he'd be relieved to have such a reminder of his youthful indiscretion that resulted in a tragedy removed from his presence."

My cousin and I stepped out of the car and started to walk towards the banquet hall attached to the firehouse. "That's what I mean. If Jim killed Ivan, I don't believe he'd be honoring him by postponing bingo night, and he certainly wouldn't lower the flag in his memory."

I shoved the strap of my Michael Kors black faux leather bag up my shoulder. I had to agree with Candie. The way Jim was reacting to Ivan's death wasn't what I thought a murderer would do. Did this place him further down on my suspect list? Maybe. But it didn't do anything to help erase me from it. Then again maybe this was all a clever act on Jim's part to throw suspicion away from himself.

We followed a line of people toward the banquet hall. Gladys and Helen were in front of us and appeared to be bickering about something, as usual. I smiled. Knowing them, it could be the color of bingo chips being used tonight during the games.

A din of voices swept out the glass door as I pulled it open, and we stepped into the building. Bright lights lent a cheery vibe to the cinder block room. It was often rented out for community events that were too small for the Civic Center. Weddings, graduation parties, and baby showers were often held in this hall. Last year, Lucy Foster even hosted a rug hooking event here. The building provided much-needed extra income for the fire company.

I'd never attended Bingo Night before, so I stood just inside the door and scanned the room. I nudged Candie's arm. "Over there. That's where we get our bingo cards and chips. Oops, I'm sorry," I said as the person behind me bumped into me trying to get into the room. I guess I was blocking the door.

Candie and I edged our way through the crowd and approached the table set up to purchase the bingo cards. On my way, I waved to a number of people I knew—Roberta Holden and her husband Clyde, Penny Richards from the library, and of course Gladys and Helen. Finally, we made it to the table selling the bingo cards. I was surprised to see Drew Ellis behind the table. Packets of bingo cards with wide markers sat in front of him. I guess I shouldn't have been, since he was a fireman. He seemed to be everywhere I went nowadays. Even at an event where a murder occurred.

"Ladies, how many packets would you like?" he asked, pointing to the bingo cards.

"I guess one. Will that be enough for the night? This is our first time here," I said.

Drew, his blond hair slightly tousled, smiled at us. "Well, some folks play multiple cards at a time. Since you're new, I'd suggest one card at a time until you get the hang of things. Jim calls a pretty fast game, and it might take time to get used to the speed he goes."

Candie picked up a packet and shook it. "Where are the bingo chips?"

Drew laughed. "That's what the marker is for. We don't use chips anymore. Just dab the marker on a square if it's one Jim calls."

Candie shook her head. "The whole world is changing too fast. Even bingo isn't the same as we used to play when we were kids."

"How much for one packet?" I asked, digging into my purse for my wallet.

"Five dollars," Drew said, extending his hand for my money.

Candie drew her wallet out, too, still mumbling how even the game of bingo wasn't safe from changing times. She handed Drew her money. He thanked us and wished us luck.

I turned towards the room and scanned it for a table with two empty chairs. The room was filling up fast.

"Yoo-hoo. Sam, over here."

I glanced in the direction of the voice calling me and saw Gladys waving a scrawny arm at me. I waved back and pointed Candie and myself in her direction.

"I saw you ladies come in and saved two seats for you. Plunk yourselves down." Gladys flicked her gnarled fingers in the direction of two empty metal chairs across from her that surrounded one of the many round tables in the gray-painted cinder block room.

"Gladys, sweetie, that was mighty kind of y'all to save us a seat." Candie looked around the room. "Ooh-wee, this certainly is a hopping place. It's busier than a half-price sale at Discount World on Black Friday."

My head swiveled, too, taking in the crowd gathered in the room. I knew the parking lot was filling up when we had arrived, but only a half an hour later, the banquet hall was packed. Seating was at a premium. From the size of the crowd, it had to include people not only from Wings Falls, but also the surrounding towns. This, I thought, was a good thing, as the money generated from the night of bingo playing would greatly help with the fire company's expenses.

"Gladys, where's Frank tonight?" I asked, noticing her Pookie Bear was absent.

"He's home watching a football game. The Jets are playing, and you know him. If the house was burning down, he wouldn't miss one of his favorite team's games," Gladys said.

I nodded. I could just imagine Frank sitting on their plastic slip-covered sofa decked out in a Jets sweatshirt with a Jets ball cap perched on his head.

Candie and I placed our bingo cards and markers on the table in front of our seats. "Before we settle down, I think I'd like a cup of coffee and a goodie to munch on. What about you, Candie?"

"That sounds right fine to me," she said, flicking her hair back over her shoulder.

We weaved our way through the crowded room towards the concession area of the hall. Behind the table covered with coffee urns, doughnuts, and pastries stood Martha Callaway.

I blinked, surprised. She certainly was involved with the fire company, even though she didn't have a relative who was an active firefighter.

"Hi, Martha. Boy, you certainly give a lot of time to the fire company. Saturday at the Civic Center, and tonight here," I said as I snagged a glazed doughnut from the table.

Martha nodded. Her blonde ponytail swayed back and forth, brushing her shoulders. "Yes, as the president of the woman's auxiliary, I feel I should be here."

"That's very admirable. I don't know many women who would give up their time like you do, and especially with all the responsibilities you have." I grabbed a paper cup and poured myself a cup of coffee.

"Yes, but my grandpop was a member of this fire company. He and I were very close, so I do it as a tribute to him and to show Jaxson that a person should give back to their community when they can," Martha said.

"That was such good news about Jaxson doing better." I pulled my wallet out of my purse to pay for my goodies.

"Yes, we are so very thankful. Now I can resume my teaching position and start getting a paycheck again."

I stepped aside so Candie could pay for her coffee and Danish pastry. When the cash register opened, I noticed it was overflowing with bills. My thoughts whirled back to the question as to whether she killed Ivan because he caught her pocketing money on Saturday at the Civic Center.

CHAPTER THIRTY-TWO

———

I shared my mental ramblings with Candie as we weaved our way through the crowded room back to our seats. "So, what do you think? Could she have possibly killed Ivan Saturday night?"

Candie shrugged her shoulders. "I hate to admit it, but it is a possibility. You did see how upset she became when she was talking to Ivan at the Civic Center on Saturday. If her eyes were lasers, she'd have fried him on the spot. She is probably desperate for money to pay her bills. What with having to take a leave of absence from her teaching job to take care of her son, I'm sure she didn't get her usual salary, and volunteering here at the fire hall doesn't pay any money."

Unfortunately, I had to agree with my cousin. As much as I liked Martha and thought Jaxson was adorable, Hank once told me that good people sometimes did bad things. Who knows. Maybe if I were in her situation, I'd have done the same thing. I wasn't going to judge her.

"Look, you gold digger, how many times do I have to tell you to leave my nephew alone?"

I turned in the direction of the shrill voice issuing the command. Helen. Sunny Foxx stood next to Drew Ellis. Helen, with her hands on her ample hips, towered over the table where Candie and I had purchased our bingo cards earlier. What was with this woman? Drew was certainly old enough to manage his own social life. He had to be in his late twenties or early thirties. In fact, by the red crawling up his neck, I'd say he was rather embarrassed by Helen's actions. Sunny looked equally as uncomfortable.

"Aunt Helen, please, I'm capable of running my own life. If you'll excuse me, I have a job to do, and Sunny is helping me." With that, Drew took hold of Sunny's hand and whispered something into her ear. He then turned to the next person in line and inquired as to how many bingo cards they wanted to purchase.

"The ungrateful upstart," Helen said as she stomped through the crowd, bumping people out of her way.

With a puzzled look on my face, I glanced at Candie. "What was that all about?" A thought crossed my mind. *Gladys.* "Come on. Let's get back to the table. I'll bet Gladys knows what's up with Helen and her overprotecting her nephew, Drew. We never even knew she had a nephew until the other day."

As we weaved through the tables, I wondered what Hank was up to tonight. I had left a message for him that Candie and I were going to Bingo Night, but I hadn't heard back from him. Even though he'd been taken off the case, I knew in my heart that he was still diving into the evidence to clear my name. I was sure he didn't want our dates to be in the Big House with us separated by a plexiglass barrier and me wearing an orange outfit.

After settling down at our table and taking a bite of my doughnut and a sip of coffee, I plunged ahead, asking Gladys what she knew about the Helen and Drew situation. "Gladys, you've known Helen Garber a long time, haven't you?"

Gladys's green curls bobbled about her head. "That old ninny? You bet I have. Why do you ask?"

"Because she seems to have a big dislike for Ivan Kline and equally so for Sunny Foxx. Candie and I were standing near the table selling the bingo cards, and she was reaming Drew out for being with Sunny. Oh, and Helen never mentioned having a brother, let alone a nephew, before. What's up with that?" I asked, taking another sip of my coffee.

Candie sat beside me, enjoying her coffee and Danish as I questioned Gladys.

Gladys spread her bingo cards out in front of her. She had to be playing at least three at a time. How would she be able to keep up with the number calling? I'd be lucky to find the numbers on one card. "Yes, she has a brother, Drew's father. It all goes back to when Drew was a small boy. His mother left him for another man."

Candie dabbed at the corners of her mouth. "Let me guess. That man was Ivan Kline?"

Gladys nodded. "Yep, but back then, you kept such things as quiet as possible. Not like nowadays, when people shout all their dirty laundry from the rooftop."

My eyes widened. "Wow, no wonder she had no love lost for Ivan, but would she kill him because of it? I mean, that was ages ago."

"Drew's father got over it, but a few years back, Ivan bought the lakefront property next to Drew's dad," Gladys said, studying her cards.

"Oh, my. That certainly must have tied a knot in Drew's papa's tail," Candie said, swiping Danish crumbs from her lips.

"You can say that again. They've been feuding ever since," Gladys said. She tapped the card in the middle. "This is a winner. I can feel it in my bones."

I remembered what Hank had said about the police being called to both men's residences. Things certainly weren't happy valley on the lake between these two men. Would Drew have placed the blame on Ivan for his mother abandoning him all those many years ago and killed him? He seemed pretty smitten with Sunny Foxx. Maybe he saw her and Ivan together at the ball and had visions of Ivan stealing another woman away from him, and he snapped. Love can do strange things to people. Some very irrational things at times.

"So why is Helen so upset with Drew being with Sunny? He's a big boy now. He has to be in his late twenties or early thirties at least." I pulled a piece off my glazed doughnut and placed it in my mouth, savoring the rich sweetness on my tongue.

Gladys tapped her marker on the tabletop. "Well, when Drew's mom first walked out on him, Helen stepped in to take care of the boy. Drew's dad remarried a couple of years later, but you know Helen… She didn't give up the role as his surrogate mother lightly. She still feels she has a say in his life."

"Yeah, I can see that happening with her," I said. Boy, could I. "But why the big secret all these years about her having a brother and Drew being her nephew?"

Gladys shrugged her thin shoulders. "Helen thought of Drew's mom leaving as a big family scandal. One that had to be kept quiet at all costs. I pity the poor woman who Drew finally marries. She'd better be able to stand up to Helen, or she'll rule their life."

I almost felt sorry for Sunny. If her relationship with Drew became serious, she'd better make sure her backbone was made of steel. Right now, Sunny had more serious things to deal with, like ridding herself of her abusive husband. One good thing, for me at least, was her attention was off of Hank. I knew that was being selfish, but one cheating relationship in my life was enough to last me a lifetime.

Candie pointed to my packet of bingo cards with a ruby red–painted fingernail. "Open up your packet and spread out your cards. It's almost seven thirty, and the games should start soon."

I glanced up at the large round clock mounted on the wall to the left of a small stage. Set up at the front of the stage was a podium. A circular wire cage holding small wooden, numbered bingo balls sat on a table next to it. In a few minutes, Jim Turner would mount the stage and spin the cage and pull out the winning numbers. I spied Jane Burrows, not a hair out of place of her pixie haircut. She was back to wearing her twin sweater sets and khaki pants. Tonight, the sweater set was Kelly green, bright enough to rival Gladys's hair color. She climbed the steps to the stage and placed a bottle of water on the podium. I figured she must be Jim's assistant tonight. If she used the same organizational skills here that she did at the library, things would run smoothly. Or at least, I hoped they would.

I studied my three bingo cards and marker spread out before me. Should I play them all at once or use one card per game? Because this was my first go at playing bingo since I was a child, I thought I'd ease into the world of bingo with one card a game. I leaned over and told Candie my plan of attack.

"Child, you have no sense of adventure. I'm going to go all in and play three at a time. If I can handle that, which I'm sure I can, I'll purchase more cards for the other games."

I smiled at Candie. She'd been a daredevil since the day she was born. I often wished I had her bravery and spunk, but such is life, and Hank loved me the way I was.

"Ladies and gentlemen, welcome to Bingo Night at the Wings Falls Firehouse." A round of applause greeted Jim as he spoke into the microphone. I hadn't noticed him approach the podium. I guess I was too engrossed in planning my bingo-playing strategy.

"Is everyone ready for a fun night?"

A round of applause and shouts greeted him.

I certainly was, especially after this past weekend. I wanted to put Sunny, Martha, Drew, Jim, Helen, and all the other murder suspects out of my mind for the evening. Especially thoughts of me on that list. As I glanced across the table at Gladys holding her bingo card marker in a death grip over her cards, A mangy-looking rabbit's foot sat on the table next to them. I knew there was no way she'd have killed Ivan either.

CHAPTER THIRTY-THREE

———

"Candie, this could become an addiction. I may have to join Bingo Players Anonymous," I said after playing my tenth game of bingo. I hadn't won any games yet, but it wasn't from lack of trying. My Coach wallet was going home a lot lighter after I'd bought my fourth set of cards. I rationalized it was all for a good cause, the fire company.

Now, my cousin was a different story. She had won a gift card for dinner at Momma Mia's. Many of the local businesses donated gift cards or items from their stores as prizes.

Candie laughed at me. "I know what you mean. It is quite habit forming, but Mark will be thrilled at this gift card to eat out at Momma Mia's." When she waved the card at me, I stuck my tongue out at her. She laughed. "Sore loser."

I joined in her laughter then nodded towards where Drew sat with Sunny at the table selling the bingo cards. "In spite of what Helen said earlier this evening, she's keeping him company."

"Good for her. Shows she's not going to back down to blustery ol' Helen. Oh, my. Look who has walked up to their table. That skanky-looking fellow from the library parking lot."

I glanced over. Sunny's husband. "What's he doing here?"

"You can bet he's up to no good. Any man who'd hurt a woman is a low-down pole cat in my mind. Come on. Let's see what he wants." Candie pushed her chair back from the table.

"Wait. I think I should phone Hank about this." I reached into my purse and pulled out my phone. Sunny's husband had a scowl on his face. He didn't appear to be here for a game of bingo.

"Good idea," Candie said, not waiting for me.

"Where's she off to?" Gladys asked, stacking her pile of bingo cards.

There was a lull in the bingo games. Jim had announced an intermission. He pointed to the tables ladened with pies, cakes, cookies, and more and urged the players to partake of the goodies prepared by the Woman's Auxiliary.

I tapped Hank's number on my phone and crossed my fingers that he would pick up. I held my finger up to Gladys, motioning that I'd be with her in a minute.

Relief spread through me as Hank answered on the second ring. "Hank, it's me. I wanted to let you know that Sunny's husband has showed up here at Bingo Night at the fire hall." I had told him earlier of Candie's and my encounter with him at the library. "Okay, I'll see you in a few minutes."

I hung up from Hank and turned to Gladys. I pointed to Sunny's husband and related to Gladys what had happened at the library with him.

"Why that scallywag. He should be tarred and feathered then run out of town for treating a woman that way. I'm going to give him a piece of my mind." Gladys rose from her chair.

I got up and hurried after her. The two of us joined Candie at the bingo card table. So far, I hadn't heard any heated conversation between Drew, Sunny, and her husband.

"Alex, please, just leave me alone. Understand that I'm not coming back to you. Our marriage is over." Tears streamed down Sunny's face.

"But what about Carter? You can't keep me from seeing my son." The pleading tone in Alex's voice almost made me feel sorry for him, but then I thought of how he had treated Sunny at the library and my spine stiffened.

Sunny jutted out her chin. She wasn't about to back down to Alex's whining. She was in full Momma Bear mode. "You know the judge said that until you can prove you are seriously trying to kick your drug habit, you can't be around him."

Candie stood next to me with her arms crossed, glaring at Alex. From the set of her jaw, I knew it was all she could do hold her tongue and not give this fellow a piece of her mind.

"Buddy, I think you should move along. Sunny obviously doesn't want you here," Drew said, his arm around Sunny.

Alex brushed a lock of greasy hair out of his eyes and puffed out his chest. His clothes were the same he'd been wearing the other day. It was all I could do not to gag as I breathed in the sour smell that wafted from them.

Alex took a step towards Drew. "I don't know who you are, but you'll be sorry if you try to take my lady from me."

A hand clamped on to Alex's shoulder. "I think you should take this fireman's advice and leave."

I turned to see Hank towering over Alex by a good four inches. A serious *don't mess with me* look on his face.

Alex swiveled towards Hank and raised a hand as if to knock Hanks's off his shoulder. "Buddy, get your hand off of me."

With his free hand, Hank reached into the inner pocket of his sport coat and pulled out his badge. I smiled at his Incredible Hulk tie. Alex would do well to obey Hank's order, or I feared Hank would release his inner green superhero on him.

Alex's skin paled even lighter than its sickly pallor, if that was possible, when he glimpsed Hank's badge. He shifted from foot to foot. "Ummm, no need to have called the police on me. I was only trying to talk to my wife, here." He nodded towards Sunny.

"Soon-to-be ex," she corrected him.

"Well, you've had your say, and I think it's time for you to leave. I don't think this lady wants to continue this conversation. Am I right, Ms. Foxx?" Hank asked, turning his gaze to her.

Sunny nodded. Her blonde hair swayed about her shoulders as she swiped tears from her cheeks. "You're correct, Detective Johnson. Thank you for coming to my aid."

Hank smiled. "All in a day's work, ma'am." He nodded at me. "I'll see you later," he said as he turned to lead Alex out of the banquet hall.

"Wow, he's really something when he's in his official police mode," Candie said.

"Yep, he's my superhero." I was so very proud of him. He'd quickly defused what could have been a messy situation.

"You're lucky to have found such a fine fellow. I wish I had used my head instead of my emotions when I met Alex. Only good thing to have come from our marriage is Carter. I hope I haven't scarred him too much having Alex as his father," Sunny said, dabbing at her eyes with a torn tissue.

Drew pulled her next to him. "Second time will be the charm."

I had heard of love at first sight but had never witnessed it before. It looked to me like Drew had a bad case of it. He had fallen, and fallen hard, for Sunny. I hoped she returned his affections. Although with the murder of Ivan still not solved, could one of them be a murderer? Was Sunny so desperate to be rid of Alex that she'd hook up with any available male? Maybe, knowing that Ivan was single, she thought he'd be a good candidate for Alex's replacement, even if he was old enough to be her father. Stranger things had happened. I wasn't about to scratch her off my suspect list yet.

"Do you want to get another coffee before we sit back down for some serious bingo playing?"

I laughed. I'd be lucky if I ever saw Candie on bingo nights again. She'd be here at the firehouse.

"Sure," I said to her question. I turned to Gladys, who had remained surprisingly quiet through the Alex ordeal. "Do you want to join us?"

Her green curls bobbled as she shook her head. "No, I want to get settled in my seat and study my cards. Jim will be calling numbers soon. I'll see you back at the table."

"Okay. We'll only be a few minutes." I watched as Gladys made her way back to our table. I knew she was spry for her age, but it was a crowded room and she could stumble on a chair leg.

I glanced over at Sunny and Drew. The crowd that had gathered to witness the disagreement between Alex and Sunny was now replaced by people seeking to buy more bingo cards. "Everything okay here?"

Drew and Sunny nodded in unison. Sunny gave me a weak smile. "Yes, and thank you for calling Hank. I presume it was you who summoned him, right?"

"I confess, it was me. It didn't look like Alex was up to any good, so I gave him a call."

"I can't thank you enough." A faint blush colored her cheeks. "I want to apologize if you thought there was anything between Hank and me. He told me early on that he was in a committed relationship with you. I've made such a mess with my life that sometimes I don't know why I act the way I do" She gazed over at Drew. "But I think I'm on the right track now and am getting my head and heart straightened out."

Drew squeezed her hand.

"That's great. We'd better go fetch our cups of coffee. We're blocking people from buying their bingo cards from you," I said, glancing in the direction of the refreshment tables.

A tapping sound came over the PA system. I turned towards the stage to see Jane leaning in towards the microphone. "Folks, get your cards ready. We'll resume playing in about five minutes."

Candie tugged at my sleeve. "Come on. Let's get our coffee and go back to our seats."

Boy, was she ever on a mission.

"Where's that lowlife, Jim Turner, who ruined my life and murdered my brother?"

CHAPTER THIRTY-FOUR

———

Heads whipped around towards the loud voice, wanting to know where Jim was. Silence descended on the fire hall. You could hear a bingo card drop.

The crowd parted as the voice's owner walked farther into the hall. The fellow looked to be about Hank's height of six-foot, but that's where any similarity to a "normal"-looking male ended. The fellow's face was a mass of red scars. He wore a black patch over his left eye. Hair was missing from the front of his scalp. While his right hand that jutted out from his green canvas jacket appeared to be normal with all five fingers intact, his left hand was a fleshy stump except for his thumb and pointer finger. All of this was disconcerting, but what troubled me the most was the lighter he carried in his right hand and the bundle of sparklers he grasped in what remained of his left.

"Jim Turner, you cowardly dog, show your face. It's Kaleb Kline. Remember me? The sap you maimed all those years ago."

Candie leaned over to me and whispered, "So, it's true what we read on the computer at the library. Jim must have been involved in a teenage accident involving Ivan's brother."

I shook my head. "It appears so. Hank must still be in the parking lot or at least nearby. I'll see if I can text him to come back as soon as possible. This looks like it could turn ugly, especially as crowded as this hall is." I pulled my phone out of my jeans pocket and flipped it open, With shaking fingers, I texted Hank about what was going on in the fire hall and for him to return or at least alert someone to come here.

Jim stepped into the open on the stage. "'Kaleb, it has been a long time. You know I've regretted every day the foolish game we were playing with sparklers when we were teens. I'm sorry you're the one who got injured, but we were all willing participants. I kept my end of the bargain and did the community service the judge handed down to us. I've tried to live a life of giving back ever since then. But it seems you didn't uphold your part of the bargain by not naming who partook in our prank."

Jim looked out over the sea of faces staring up at him. "Yes, folks. Back when I was a teenager, a group of us young men did a very foolish thing in challenging ourselves to our version of hot potato, only that time we tied a bunch of sparklers together and tossed it around to each other. In our ignorance, we thought they would fizzle out when it came to the last person, but unfortunately the bundle exploded when it got to Kaleb. As you can see, it did a lot of damage to the poor fellow."

Out from the side of the stage walked Jane. She walked up to Jim and slid an arm around his waist.

He patted her arm. "Jane, go back to the side of the stage. I don't want you to get hurt. This is between Kaleb and me."

Jane shook her head and ran a hand through her short pixie cut hair. She reached up and laid the palm of her hand on Jim's cheek. "No, Jim, I'm staying right here by your side. If it concerns you, it concerns me,"

I tugged at Candie's arm and blinked back tears. "That is true love."

Candie sniffled. "I agree. Jane may have found love late in life like you and me, but better late than never."

I thought about how much I loved Hank and couldn't agree with her more.

A sneer crossed Kaleb's disfigured face. "Awww, how touching. She loves you, Jim. With a mug like mine, how many girls do you think have given me a second look over the years? Let's see how much she'll care about you once you have your face fried off of you." A flame sprang to life as Kaleb flicked the lighter. As if in slow motion, Kaleb's hand moved towards the bundle of sparklers.

"Kaleb, don't do it," Jim shouted. "One tragedy is enough, I regret what happened all those years ago, but harming others won't change things, and it won't bring your brother back. I didn't kill him. I swear I didn't. If it makes you feel better, you and I can play that game of toss the sparklers outside. I'll make sure I'm the loser this time. But please, not in here with all of these innocent folks." He pulled away from Jane and started towards the steps of the stage.

"No, Jim!" Don't do it!" Jane screamed. Tears streamed down her face.

"Umph," I said. I lost my balance and stumbled against Candie as Drew barreled past us into Kaleb. He knocked the lighter and bundle of sparklers out of Kaleb's hand as they hit the floor.

The crowd, which had been quieter than church mice while all this had been taking place between Kaleb and Jim, came to life.

Gladys jumped out of her seat and whipped off the silk scarf she had worn around her neck. She handed it to Drew, who sat astride a squirming Kaleb. "Here. Use this to tie his hands together."

Jim jumped off the stage and ran to Drew. With his help, they subdued Kaleb, binding his arms with Gladys's scarf.

Gladys walked over to Candie and me. "Good thinking, Gladys, " I said.

"*Humph.* I just want him out of here so we can get on with our bingo games."

I laughed. Gladys sure had her priorities straight.

The door to the bingo hall burst open, and in strode Joe Peters. It wasn't often that I welcomed the sight of him, but this was one time I did. I guessed Hank was still tied up with Alex, so he phoned in the need for help at the fire hall to the station.

Joe strode over to Drew. He pushed back his jacket and rested his hand on the butt of his gun. "Drew Ellis, I'm taking you down to the station for questioning in the murder of Ivan Kline."

My eyes about bugged out of my head. I shook a finger in my ear to make sure I was hearing Joe correctly. Wasn't he here because of my text message to Hank about Kaleb Kline?

"Did I hear Sandy correctly? He wants to take Drew to the station for questioning in Ivan's murder? Can't he see there is another situation going on right now that needs his attention? I know Hank keeps telling me Joe's a good officer, but really?" I pointed to Kaleb lying on the floor of the banquet hall, trussed up like a Thanksgiving turkey with Gladys's scarf.

Jim stepped forward. "Officer Peters, you may not have noticed"—he nodded to Kaleb's prone body—"but the gentleman on the floor tried to blow up this banquet hall along with its fine citizens. You may want to attend to that situation first, and then I'm sure Mr. Ellis would be glad to answer any question you might have."

Joe blinked. "Blow this place up? I never got a call about any trouble at the fire hall."

I stepped forward. "I sent Hank a text concerning what was happening here. I thought that was the reason why you showed up."

Joe furrowed his unibrow. "Nope, I have a warrant here to take Mr. Ellis in for questioning. Don't know anything about what was going down here."

Jim nodded then proceeded to fill him in on the events that happened, from the time Kaleb entered the banquet hall until Drew tackled him, saving the evening from a total disaster.

Heads nodded as Jim related what had transpired. Folks stepped forward to second Jim's story.

Kaleb, who had been lying on the tile flooring sobbing like a baby while all this was going on, struggled against the scarf restraining his hands.

Joe bent and pulled Kaleb to his feet.

He stood before Joe, his scarred face drenched in tears, blubbering about how unfair life was.

Joe swept the room with his leather-gloved hand. "Is what's been said here true? You tried to blow these folks to smithereens?"

Kaleb hiccupped. "No. Just him for killing my brother, Ivan." He nodded his head towards Jim.

"He couldn't have killed your brother, as he was with me all night."

CHAPTER THIRTY-FIVE

———

My jaw dropped as Jane stepped forward to make this bold statement. I knew she and Jim were seeing each other, but I didn't know they were *that* serious. Good for her. But then I remembered at the Fireman's Ball she had said she needed to go home and check on her mom, who wasn't feeling well. Jim said he'd return to the Ball after he dropped her off.

I turned to Candie and shared my thoughts with her. "Did you see Jim after he left with Jane? Did he come back to the Civic Center?"

Candie's brow furrowed as she mulled over my questions. "Now that you mention it, I didn't see him again Saturday night. Do you suppose that after checking in on her mom, they decided to shack up together?"

I swatted at her arm. "Don't be so crude. It's obvious they're in love. You know how that is."

A dreamy look came over Candie's face. "Yeah, I do."

In spite of the situation happening around us, I couldn't help but smile. I had a feeling that Mark was winning Dixie over to his side again with all the YouTube advice we had gathered on building a relationship with a cat.

Jane stood by Jim. He placed an arm around her shoulder and pulled her close to him. "You don't have to say anything more. This can all be sorted out at the police station if need be." He bent and placed a tender kiss on the top of her head.

I felt positive that what Jane had said was true. There went Jim as one of my suspects if he had spent the night with Jane. That left Martha, Drew, Sunny, maybe even Helen, from the snide remarks she'd said about Ivan wrecking her brother's life. Of course, there was also Gladys and me, but Peters did say he was here for Drew and not Kaleb.

Joe spoke into the mic attached to the shoulder of his jacket. He turned to the crowd. "I don't want anyone going anywhere. I've called for backup, and they will be here any minute to take your statements about what happened here tonight. In the meantime, Mr. Ellis, I have a few questions for you regarding your whereabouts on Saturday night." He pointed to a vacant chair. "Mr. Kline, sit your sorry bones down there until my guys get here and deal with you."

His head hanging down, Kaleb sat in the chair as directed. He looked resigned to his fate.

Joe now focused his attention on Drew. "Mr. Ellis, are you a smoker?"

Drew nodded his head in reply.

I knew his answer to be the truth since I'd seen him smoking at the four-wheeler races earlier in the day on Saturday. I wondered what that had to do with Ivan's death.

Joe pulled a small notebook out of the inner pocket of his jacket. He flipped it open. "Do you smoke…?" he asked, mentioning a popular brand of cigarettes.

Again, Drew nodded.

A smirk crossed Joe's pudgy face. "Turn around, please." Joe unsnapped the leather case that held his handcuffs. "I'm arresting you for the murder of Ivan Kline."

Drew swayed. "I didn't do it. What evidence do you have that says I killed him?"

If possible, the smirk on Joe's face widened. "A cigarette butt with your fingerprints on it was found at the scene of the crime."

A gasp was heard behind me. I turned to see Sunny standing there, clutching a stack of bingo cards in her hands, and then I saw Helen pushing her way through the crowd of bingo players.

"Joe Peters, take those handcuffs off my nephew right now. He didn't murder that poor excuse of a human being, Ivan Kline." Helen came to a halt before Joe. She planted herself mere inches from him.

Joe puffed up his chest. I didn't think you could slip one of the night's bingo cards between them. "Mrs. Garber, you are interfering with an official police investigation. Please move back, or I will have to arrest you, too."

Helen poked an orange-painted nail in Joe's chest. "Drew was at my house Saturday night after the Fireman's Ball."

Joe chuckled. "Yeah, right. As if a red-blooded male would spend a Saturday night with you instead of some hot chick. Like I believe that one."

Helen huffed out a breath, stirring a loose strand of flaming red hair that had escaped her French twist. "If you must know, when the Ball ended, my car wouldn't start so he gave his uncle Orville and me a ride home. His uncle invited him in to watch a wrestling match he'd taped from earlier in the evening. They enjoyed a couple of beers while watching the match, so I convinced him to sleep over in our spare bedroom instead of driving home."

"How do I know you're not trying to cover up for him? I'm sure you'd lie to keep him out of jail." Joe jutted out his chin, He wasn't about to back down from Helen.

Helen sucked in a breath. Her face turned almost as red as her hair. Oh, my. Joe had done it now when he called Helen a liar. I could almost see the steam pouring out of her ears.

"Call Pizza Heaven if you want proof. They have an all-night pizza delivery. About one in the morning, Orville and Drew felt like having a pizza with their beer. Drew answered the door and paid the delivery guy."

Joe deflated like a balloon after Helen offered proof that Drew spent the night at her house.

Joe grumbled under his breath. "All right, it looks like you have an alibi." He unlocked the handcuffs then turned his attention to Kaleb, who stood next to Officer Reed, who had arrived moments before to assist in questioning the bingo crowd.

Sunny strolled up to Drew and placed a hand on his arm while he rubbed his wrists that moments before were encased in handcuffs. "I knew you were innocent. You're too kind to hurt anyone."

Drew gazed at Sunny with pure adoration in his eyes. Helen glared at them both. Moments before, she had defended her nephew like a momma lion would its cubs, but now I wondered if she regretted her decision, seeing him with Sunny. She huffed and turned to walk back to her seat.

"Thank you, Aunt Helen," Drew called after her.

"Whatever," she said, waggling her finger at him over her shoulder.

The officers had finished taking statements from various bingo players. They thanked everyone for their cooperation and left.

Joe had already left to transport Kaleb to the Wings Falls Police station.

The room was buzzing with excitement over the evenings activities. The players got way more than an evening of bingo.

Out of the corner of my eye, I spied Jim walking across the stage and up to the microphone. "Folks, the night is still young. Do you all want to continue playing bingo?"

Hoots and hollers rang out and echoed off the cinder block walls in affirmative.

Over her head Gladys waved the scarf that had been returned to her when real handcuffs had been placed on Kaleb. "You bet your sweet bippy," she shouted out.

Candie looked at me and mouthed, *What?*

Gladys saw her. "You youngsters missed out on all the good television shows. It's a line from a classic show in the late sixties, *Laugh-In.* They don't make them like they did then. Now everything is drama, drama, drama."

I did have to agree with her. Maybe that's why if Hank isn't over or I'm not working on my next Porchop book or hooking on a rug, I'd rather curl up on the sofa with a good mystery and a glass of wine.

Jim tapped the mic to get everyone's attention. Jane had walked to the front of the stage. I blinked at what she was carrying. A teddy bear that had to be at least three feet tall.

"Folks, the prize for this game is this adorable teddy bear, donated by the Toy Box situated on Main Street. Be sure to patronize them for your young friends."

As Jim talked, Jane ran her hand over the teddy ala Vanna White style. I knew where the Toy Box was situated on Main but had never had any need to shop there.

Jim called out the numbers, and ten minutes later, I was the proud owner of the teddy bear.

Candie laughed. "Now what are you going to do with that teddy? He's a little too big for Porkchop to play with."

I had to agree with her. "Yeah, I'd be afraid if it fell on him, Porkchop would suffocate. Why couldn't I have won a gift certificate to one of Wings Falls fine restaurants like you did?"

I smacked her arm as a smug smile spread across her face. "Just not as lucky as me, I guess."

I walked up to the stage to claim my prize. As I returned to my seat, I had to pass by the table selling the coffee and doughnuts. A thought flashed through my brain. I knew who the perfect recipient of this large teddy would be.

CHAPTER THIRTY-SIX

————

I struggled to shove the teddy bear into the back seat of my Bug. He was bigger than I thought.

Candie pointed to her Mustang parked in my driveway next to my car. "Are you sure you don't want to take Precious? There would be a lot more room for Teddy, Porkchop, and the two of us."

I stopped in mid push to consider her question. My cousin was right, but I was being stubborn. No way was a three-foot-tall stuffed bear going to outwit me. This was war between the bear and me, and I was going to win. I placed my shoulder up against the bear and sucked in my breath. With one last mighty shove, the bear settled into the Bug's back seat. I backed out of my car and gave Candie a high-five. I had won the battle between the bear and me.

I brushed the hair that had fallen over my forehead out of my eyes, straightened my coat, and turned to Candie. "I'm going in the house to fetch Porkchop. Settle in the front seat so I can have you hold Porkie while I drive us over to Martha Callaway's house."

Candie saluted me. "Yes, sir. Right away, sir."

I stuck my tongue out at her. "You're such a smartie pants. I don't know why I put up with your sass."

A beatific smile spread across Candie's face. "Because you love me."

I laughed. She knew me way too well. "It's a good thing we're related, or you'd be minus one friend."

Candie glanced at the bejeweled watch encircling her slim wrist. "We'd better get over to Martha's. I told Mark I'd be in the office before noon, and it's nine thirty right now." She tapped the face of her watch with a fingernail.

"Okay, I'll be right out with Porkchop." I traipsed up my snow-covered sidewalk. A small snowstorm had blown through last night, leaving about three inches of new snow on the ground for me to deal with. I groaned. Spring and warmer weather couldn't come soon enough.

Within minutes, I was back at my car. "Here and be careful. He's precious cargo." I handed Porkchop over to Candie. He sported a black and red checked turtleneck sweater to ward off the cold. My cousin settled Porkie on her lap then turned to me and gave me the stink eye.

"Okay, so tell me again… What is this plan of yours with Martha Callaway?" Candie asked, cradling my dog next to her purple fleece coat. Porkchop snuggled into it, loving the feel of the soft material.

"Well, when I won the teddy bear last night, I thought, what a better opportunity to quiz Martha than to come offering a gift to her son." I put the Bug in reverse and backed out of my driveway. While my sidewalk may have been covered with snow, the town's snowplows had already been down my street and eliminated any evidence of last night's snowfall off the roads.

Candie stroked the top of Porkchop's head. "What is that old saying? Beware of Greeks bearing gifts. Is that us—the Greeks bringing a fake gift to a little boy?"

Now that my cousin put it that way, I felt lower than a worm and about as slimy. "I hadn't thought of it that way. It is kind of underhanded, but what am I to do? I've got to prove I'm innocent."

Candie reached over and patted my hand that gripped the steering wheel. "I know, sugar. I wish this whole nasty mess would go away."

I leaned closer to the front window. The defroster in my car was going full blast trying to keep up with the cold air outside. I rubbed a circle in the fog on the windshield, trying to peer out. "Look for Bay Street. It should be coming up soon."

"How did you find out where she lives?" Candie glanced out of the side window.

"I googled her name, and it popped up on the internet. It's 47 Bay Street," I said, still straining to see out my fog-covered front window.

Candie laughed. "Not much is secret nowadays. You can find anyone on the internet."

Porkchop stirred on her lap. He lifted his head and opened one eye to see what was so funny then settled back down and fell back to sleep.

"There! There! Turn right there." Candie bounced with excitement as she pointed out the street sign.

I slowed down, put my blinker on, and turned down the street Candie had pointed to.

I drove slowly down the leafless tree-lined street. I could imagine it in the spring when the leaves budded out. They would provide plenty of shade for the children playing on this street. Number 47 was at the end of the street. I turned the car into the driveway of a charming Cape Cod style red brick home. The mailbox at the end of the drive was in the shape of a white bunny rabbit. Dormant flower beds lined the flag stone walkway leading to the house. Come spring, I was sure they would be filled with a riot of color.

I placed the Bug in park and exited the car. Porkchop and Candie got out of the passenger side. Candie clutched Porkchop's leash in one hand and straightened her jacket with the other. I flipped back my seat and tugged on the teddy bear's arm. After a few tugs, he popped out of the back seat, catching me off balance. It was all I could do to keep from landing on my rear with a teddy bear sitting on top of me.

I grabbed Teddy around the waist and started up the sidewalk. "Can you handle Porkchop?"

Candie nodded and followed me toward the house. It looked like Martha had been up early clearing her sidewalk of snow.

I pushed on the doorbell attached to the house next to the storm door. A buzzing sound rang inside the house.

I heard small feet scrambling towards the door. "I'll get it, Momma."

"Jaxson, what did I say about opening the door to strangers? You wait up for me."

I smiled. Youth were so trusting. I wish they could remain that way forever, but unfortunately life wasn't so kind.

The door swung open. I was sure Martha had checked to see who stood on the other side of the peephole in the middle of the front door before she swung it open. "Sam, Candie, what brings you here?"

Porkchop barked at our feet. Martha looked down and laughed. "And of course you, Porkchop. I'm sorry I missed you."

His whole body shook as he wagged his tail.

"Momma, look! He's the doggie we met at the library." An excited Jaxson bounced from foot to foot. He bent to pat Porkchop's back. Porkchop in turn licked his hand. Jaxson giggled. "He's kissing me, Momma."

"Yes, he is, sweetheart," Martha said. Her blonde hair was scraped back into a ponytail. A dish towel hung over her shoulder. She rubbed her hands down slim-fitting jeans.

"Hi, Jaxson, Martha. I hope this isn't a bad time to visit, but you might remember I won this teddy bear last night at Bingo Night. I was wondering if Jaxson would like to give him a home, since I don't have any little ones living with me." I laughed and nodded towards my dog. "Other than Porkchop, and I don't think he'd know what to do with him."

Martha brushed back a stray strand of hair that had escaped her ponytail behind her ear. She looked down at Jaxson. "Jaxson, what do you think? Do you think this teddy bear would like to come live with you?"

Jaxson looked up from petting Porkchop. His eyes widened in excitement. "Really? I can have this teddy bear all for myself?"

"Really," I said. "I couldn't think of any other young man who'd love him as much as Porkchop and I would. Could you?"

"Me! Me!" Jaxson shouted.

I felt like a real heel using a small boy to possibly nail his mother for murder.

CHAPTER THIRTY-SEVEN

––––––

I held the teddy out to him. His small arms reached for the large bear that was almost as tall as him.

Martha pushed the front door open farther. "Oh please, where are my manners? I have brain fog this morning. I didn't get home until late last night after bingo. With this little one here, there's no sleeping late. Come in. I still have some coffee left in the pot. Would you care for a cup? It's decaf. My mom's here, so that's what she brews up. Her high blood pressure, you know."

Yep, I knew all right. "Thanks, Martha. That would be awfully kind of you."

I relieved Candie of Porkchop's leash. We followed Martha and a giggling Jaxson into the living room.

"Grandmom, Grandmom. Come here and see what I've got," an excited Jaxson called out.

An older woman who looked to be in her seventies entered the room, wiping her hands on a dish towel. She was well dressed in a pair of slim-fitting jeans and a flowing floral top. She wore a pair of brown leather boots on her feet I would have loved to have in my wardrobe. Her stylish gray bob swung back and forth as she laughed. "What do you have there, Jaxson?"

"This nice lady gave him to me. I love him with all my heart." Jaxson hugged the large teddy bear to his small body. His arms barely encircled the toy.

Martha pointed to the woman who I gathered was Jaxson's grandmother. "Sam, Candie, this is my mom and savior, Sophia Eddy."

Sophia blushed and waved away Martha's statement. "Oh, go on. What's family for, if not to help each other out? I get a special bonus by being able to be with my grandson. He keeps me young and on my toes. Who's this cute pup you brought with you?" she asked, pointing to Porkchop.

I swear Porkchop's ears perked up at being called cute. I held out my hand to her. "It's nice to meet you, Mrs. Eddy. I'm sure a young one like Jaxson requires a lot of energy to keep up with. This is my dog, Porkchop. Jaxson met him at the library the other day. I thought he might like a visit with Porkie without so many kids around."

"Oh, please call me Sophie. All my friends do, and for making my grandson so happy, I count you as a friend."

Geez, could I feel any rottener now using the teddy bear as a pretext to get information out of Martha. I might as well get right to the point. "Martha, I was wondering if you could answer a couple of questions I have about Ivan Kline?"

Martha, who had been watching her son pet Porkchop, snapped her head in my direction. Her eyes narrowed as if she saw right through my teddy bear ploy. She turned towards her mother. "Mom, would you please take Jaxson into the den while I talk to these ladies?"

Sophie glanced from me to Candie. I had the feeling we weren't on her friend's list any longer. "Sure, darling. Whatever you'd like. Come on Jaxson. Let's see if you can beat your grandmom at a game of Candyland."

Jaxson giggled. "I always beat you, Grandmom. Maybe Brownie can play, too."

"Brownie?" Sophie raised an eyebrow and asked.

"That's the name I'm going to call my teddy," Jaxson said as he led the way out of the room clutching Brownie.

Martha motioned towards a brown plaid sofa. "Have a seat, ladies, and ask me anything you want to know."

I sat and glanced around the room. It was nothing fancy, but it was spotless and clean. A basket of toys resided in one corner next to the television. Brass lamps sat on sturdy end tables at either end of the sofa. A rocking chair took up residence next to the fireplace. A braided rug in shades of blue covered the floor. I could feel the love embracing this home. I hated the thought of destroying that feeling. A smile curved my lips when my eyes settled on the framed pictures hanging above the fireplace of Jaxson from birth until present. A blond curly haired young boy smiled down at us. Absent where any pictures of him having lost his soft curls to his dreaded disease.

I cleared my throat. "Umm, Martha, at the Civic Center on Saturday, I noticed that you and Ivan were having words."

Martha let out a harsh laugh. "That evil man. Yes, we were. And to answer your next question, no, I didn't kill him. I might have felt like it, but no, I didn't do the deed. I'd like to shake the hand of the person who did, though."

Candie, who had remained silent since we'd entered Martha's home, let out a gasp. "Why would y'all want to kill him? Did he do something nasty to you?"

Martha shook her head. "I wish it were that simple. When Jaxson was first diagnosed with cancer, I wasn't thinking straight. The fire company was having an event where I volunteered. As you already know, I had to take a leave of absence from my teaching job to drive him to his appointments."

I sat, intent on listening to her story, I couldn't imagine what this had to do with Ivan and his death.

Martha wrung her hands together and continued. "Well, with so little cash coming in, I was short on money for my mortgage payment. I was selling Wings Falls Fire Company T-shirts and ball caps at a fire company function. They were a really hot item."

"I know you give a lot of time to the fire company," Candie said.

Martha reached down and petted Porkchop, who sat at her feet. I wondered if he was trying to lend her his moral support. "Yes, my granddad was a fireman, so I feel a connection to the company and all they do for the community."

I was getting impatient to hear where her story was leading. Would it be the proof I needed to clear me of Ivan's murder?

"Unfortunately, seeing all that money I was taking in prompted me to do a very stupid thing." Martha stared down at her hands then looked Candie and me in the eye. "I pocketed some of the money I was taking in. Ivan saw me and threatened to call the police."

A light flashed on in my brain. "So, Ivan has been blackmailing you?"

Martha shook her head. Tears trickled down her cheeks. "Luckily, I realized what I was doing and put the money back, but ever since then, he's threatened to spread the word around town that I am a thief. I could lose my job over his accusations. But if you think I killed him because of that, you're wrong. I'd lose everything I hold dear to me—Jaxson, my home, everything. I'm stronger than that. I found the best way to deal with Ivan when he made his threats was to ignore him. He had no proof. The money was all accounted for. He'd look like a fool accusing me of such a crime when no money was missing. But that didn't stop his threats, though, like Saturday at the Civic Center."

I got up from my seat and walked across the room to the wing chair she sat in. I knelt before her and placed my hands over hers. Okay, now for my zinger question. I took a deep breath then blew it out. "Martha, where were you Saturday night? I know I saw you at the Ball, but at any time did you go outside and meet with Ivan?"

Martha pulled her hands away from mine. I stood and walked back to the sofa and sat next to Candie. Porkchop followed me. He curled his long body at my feet.

"I don't know why I should answer you, but I'm innocent and don't have anything to hide. Yes, I left the ballroom for a few minutes at the end of the dance. I went down to the lower level to get a breath of fresh air and to call my mother to see how Jaxson was doing. She was babysitting him for me."

I sat quietly as she related her story.

"When I stepped outside, I saw a man and woman arguing. I called out to her to ask if everything was all right. When she turned around, I saw that it was Sunny and the gentleman was Ivan."

Candie leaned forward on the sofa. "So, Sunny was outside with Ivan." She turned to me. "I knew it. She killed Ivan."

Martha shook her head. Her ponytail swished against her shoulders. "No, there's no way she could have killed him."

CHAPTER THIRTY-EIGHT

———

Excitement coursed through me. Here was my proof that I, and Gladys, too, was innocent of Ivan's murder. Martha was eyewitness to Sunny arguing with Ivan, which must have led to her killing him. But wait… Martha had just said there was no way Sunny could have killed him. She must be wrong.

I frowned, mulling over what she had said. "What do you mean, she couldn't have murdered him? You said you saw her arguing with him."

"She couldn't have murdered him because she spent the night here with me."

My heart sank. I was back on Joe Peters' suspect list. "Why did she spend the night with you?" Maybe Sunny and Martha both killed Ivan, and this was a story they cooked up between them.

"She spent the night with me because she was too drunk to drive home. When I stepped out of the Civic Center, she and Ivan were having a pretty heated conversation. About what? From the gist of what I heard he wanted her to come home with him, and she said no. When he reached to grab her arm, I stepped between them. He fell back and bumped his head against that outhouse you Loopy Ladies had created."

That's probably how he got the bump on his head. I thought. *But what about that skillet found with Ivan's blood on it?*

"What did you do then?" Candie asked.

"The Ball was over, so I told Sunny to wait until I cleaned up my station and to come home with me for the night. She was in no condition to drive home. She mentioned that her son was staying with her uncle and gave him a quick call to tell him what her plans were. I got the feeling she didn't want to go home in the shape she was in."

My brow wrinkled in thought. "So, she spent the night with you. Can you prove that?"

Oh, my. I believed I had crossed the line with that question. Even Candie poked me in the ribs for being so bold. But, heck, my future was on the line as to whether orange was going to be the main color in my wardrobe.

"I can answer you."

I turned on the sofa in the direction of the voice. Sophie had entered the room. Jaxson held her hand while clutching the teddy bear's arm with his other hand.

"Since I knew it was going to be a late night for my daughter, I also slept over. I heard the girls when they came in and got up to make Sunny a pot of coffee."

There went my theory that either Martha or Sunny were Ivan's killers. I was back to square one. It seemed as if everyone was having a sleepover Saturday night but me. I glanced down at my snoozing pup. If only Porkchop could speak. He would vouch for me.

Jaxson ran over to his mother and climbed onto her lap.

"I did notice one strange thing when I was outside with Sunny," Martha said, hugging Jaxson to her.

Martha had my full attention. "What was that?"

"I saw an orange glow next to the building."

Candie waggled her ring-studded fingers for Martha to continue. "What do you mean, an orange glow?"

"You know, like someone was smoking, the tip of a lighted cigarette."

Drew. Could Helen have been lying about her nephew being home with her and her husband that night? Maybe Drew was hanging around outside catching a smoke when Sunny and Ivan walked outside. He could have seen the argument between them. He acts like he really cares for Sunny. Maybe he got angry at the way Ivan was treating her. Also, he had a grudge against him for destroying his family and now for causing his father property problems. Was this the tipping point, and he'd had enough and killed Ivan? Would Helen do anything, even lie to the police, to protect her nephew? She probably thought of him as a son since she cared for him when he was a small child.

I gathered up Porkchop's leash and stood. "I've taken up enough of your time. Thank you for answering my questions."

Martha placed Jaxson on the floor and stood. "You're welcome. I hope I've been helpful. Jaxson, say thank you to the kind lady for your teddy bear."

Jaxson grinned. His smile tugged at my heart. Even if I didn't get the answers I wanted, my heart warmed, knowing that I had made a little boy's day. "Thank you," he said.

"You're more than welcome. I'm glad Brownie found a good home." I turned to Candie. "You ready?"

She nodded and led the way to the door.

Porkchop settled onto the Bug's back seat while Candie and I clicked our seat belts into place.

"Well, that was a waste of time," Candie said, flipping her hair around her shoulders. "You and Gladys are still on the suspect list."

I glanced over at her. "But I did make a little boy's day with the teddy bear."

"Fat lot of good that will do you when you're sitting on your moth-eaten cot in the prison cell you'll be sharing with Big Bertha."

"Thanks a lot. You really raised my spirits," I said, shoving the key into the Bug's ignition.

"I'm just saying that we'd better dig up the killer soon, or Joe Peters will be knocking on your door with a set of bracelets, and I don't mean the rhinestone ones I wear." Candie stuck out her arm and waved her sparkly bangles at me. "Oh, can we stop at Discount World on the way home? I need to buy some more catnip toys for Dixie."

I placed the car in reverse and backed out of Martha's drive. "Sure. Is the catnip working? Does Dixie act more forgiving of Mark having taken Cuddles from her?"

"Yes, that was a brilliant idea of yours looking up on the internet for what would endear him to her. Every chance he gets, Mark plays with her and a catnip-filled toy. She hasn't hissed at him for snuggling with me on the sofa in a few days."

"That certainly is progress. How are she and Annie getting along? Still best buddies?" I pointed the Bug in the direction of Discount World.

"Yep. Still best buds," Candie replied.

Within minutes, we were in the crowded parking lot.

"Over there." Candie pointed to an empty slot.

"I'll only be a few minutes," Candie said, opening her door.

"Okay, Porkchop and I will be right here." I waved to her as she walked towards the entrance of the store.

"It sure is busy today, Porkie." He ignored me. I glanced over the back seat and saw him curled up, softly snoring. As I turned my attention towards the front of the car, I noticed a scruffy fellow approaching me. *Alex.* What would he have to say to me? I checked to make sure the car's doors were locked.

He knocked on my driver's side window and motioned for me to roll it down. Dumb, I was not. I shook my head. He didn't look happy with my response.

"Lady, I don't know who you are, but butt out of Sunny's and my business. She's my wife, and no one is going to take her from me. Understand?"

Porkchop woke up and leapt towards the front seat. He climbed onto my lap and placed his paws on the window. A fierce growl erupted from his throat. Alex backed away from my car, but not before he shook his fist at me.

CHAPTER THIRTY-NINE

———

"It's okay, Porkie. That nasty man has gone." I spent the next ten minutes trying to calm my dog and myself. I jumped in my seat when I heard a knock on the passenger window. It was Candie. I'd forgotten that I'd locked the doors because of Alex.

"What's the matter, sugar? You look as white as one of Memaw's sheets." Candie slid into her seat, clutching a Discount World bag.

I relayed to her Porkchop's and my encounter with Alex.

"Why the dirty dog. The nerve of him to threaten you that way. If I ever see him again, I'll give him a piece of my mind." Candie's voice shook with rage.

My lips turned up in a smile. I knew my cousin would tear a piece of hide off of Alex if she ever saw him again. I didn't envy him. He didn't know who he was dealing with. "He certainly wants Sunny back. It looks like she has moved on from him now that Drew is involved in her life."

Candie nodded. "I agree. I know it's early in their relationship, but both she and Drew seem quite smitten with each other."

"Yes, thank heavens she has someone to take her attention off of Hank."

Candie swatted at my arm. "Silly. Your Hank would never look at another woman. You have him hook, line, and sinker."

Warmth crawled up my neck. "The feeling is mutual. I wish we could discover who murdered Ivan so this case wouldn't be taking up so much of his time."

Candie settled her purse at her feet then turned towards me. "But I thought he was off the case and Joe Peters was handling it?"

"Technically, Joe is, but since I'm under suspicion for murdering Ivan, Hank is staying 'unofficially' involved."

"What does Joe think of that?" Candie asked.

My nerves had settled down enough from my encounter with Alex that I felt calm enough to drive Candie home. "Hank doesn't make a big deal of it, so Joe hasn't said anything. Frankly, I think Joe's grateful for any help he can get. Home?"

"Yes, it's time to feed Annie and let her out. Dixie will want some cuddling, too."

I placed Porkchop on the rear seat, started the car, and backed out of our parking space.

It was a short ten-minute drive to Candie and Mark's home. A smile always spread across my face when I pulled into their drive. Just like the house's owner, it was decked out in bling. The eaves of the house were white gingerbread trim. It wore a coat of Candie's favorite color, violet. I placed the car in park and turned to give Candie a hug goodbye.

"Come in for a cup of tea. Mark isn't home yet," Candie said, gathering up her package and purse.

I glanced back at Porkchop. He opened one of his chocolate-brown eyes at me. "What do you think, Porkie? Can you handle a few minutes with Dixie?" The two tolerated each other but kept their distance when they were together. "Annie will be home, too." Now Porkie sat up and his ears perked forward. Like Dixie, he was in love with Annie.

"Sure. I'd love to see Dixie and Annie." I slid out my door and reached in the back seat for Porkchop. We followed Candie up the front porch steps of her house. A breeze caught the wooden swing hanging from the ceiling of the porch that wrapped around the front of the house and set it on the motion. Porkchop barked when I pointed to the swing. "If I were superstitious, I'd think a ghost of the house's past owner was enjoying your swing."

Candie frowned at me. "Sugar, don't go saying such things. When I bought this house, the real estate agent said a house this old probably has a ghost or two lingering around."

I rubbed my arms as a chill raced up them. Maybe there were a few ghosts lingering around this big old house.

Candie unlocked her front door. She was immediately greeted by a barking Annie, happy to see her mistress had returned home. A puzzled look crossed Candie's face.

"What's the matter?" I asked. Porkchop barked in happiness, and his tail wagged nonstop upon seeing "his" Annie.

Candie dropped her purse and package on a small table in her entryway. "Dixie isn't here. She always meets me at the door with Annie. Dixie, Dixie. Where are you, love?" Panic filled her voice.

I unhooked Porkchop's leash and left him romping in the entryway with Annie and followed Candie into the living room. "Maybe she's sunning herself in front of a window. You know, soaking up some sun and dreaming of warmer weather coming."

Candie nodded, but I don't think my explanation reassured her very much as she went from room to room calling Dixie's name. We were in the parlor off the main living room. We'd checked every room in the large house. I'd even glanced out the window in her kitchen facing the backyard. No Dixie in sight. Candie pulled out her rhinestone-studded phone from a pocket of her coat. She punched in a number. "Mark, where was Dixie when you left the house? You didn't leave her out and forget to let her back in when you left for work, did you?" Tears clogged her throat. Suddenly her back stiffened. Her fingers gripped her phone so tight, they turned white. "No, I am not accusing you of trying to harm Dixie. I'm worried sick. I can't find her anywhere. Okay, I'll see you in a few minutes." She disconnected and tossed her phone on the lavender tufted love seat that sat nestled in a corner of the room. She turned to me with tears streaming down her smooth cheeks. "Mark said he'll be home in a few minutes to help us search for Dixie."

I placed an arm around her shoulder. "You can't possibly think he'd harm Dixie. He loves you too much to ever do such a thing, even if he and Dixie aren't BFFs. Plus, he's a good guy and would never harm an animal."

Candie shrugged out of her coat and threw it on the love seat next to her phone. She scrubbed at the tears running down her cheeks. "I know. I know. You're right. He would never harm Dixie. Even when she gave him that nasty scratch on his hand, he didn't get mad at her."

"Come on. Let's sit and wait for Mark." I settled her on the brocade-covered sofa. Being a Victorian, her house was decorated in furnishings from the era. Like Candie, they were bold and beautiful.

I glanced around the living room for Porkchop and Annie but didn't see either of them. I hoped they weren't up to any mischief in this big house.

My attention was drawn to the sound of a car screeching into the driveway. A car door slammed, and footsteps pounded up the wooden porch steps. The front door was flung open. It pounded against the wall. I hoped the etched glass in the door wouldn't break. In burst Mark. He stood in the entranceway, his tie askew. His suit jacket was missing, and the sleeves of his pristine white shirt were rolled above his elbows. From the looks of him, he'd rushed out of his office, not bothering to even don a coat against the cold temperatures outside. He scrubbed a hand over his shaved head.

"Candie, what is this all about? You mentioned Dixie is missing. How can that be? She was here when I left this morning. I gave her a handful of those cat treats you bought her the other day at the Shop and Save. You know, the ones with that tuna flavor. She licked them right out of my hand."

Candie glanced up at Mark with tears in her eyes. "Are you sure she didn't scoot out when you left for work?"

Mark walked over to the sofa. I stood so he could sit next to her. He took my seat and pulled her into his arms. "Sweetheart, I'm positive she didn't sneak out. You know how she hates the cold and won't put a paw outside until the springtime, when the weather is more to her liking."

A faint smile curved Candie's lips. She nodded. "You're right, but I can't find her. You know she and Annie always greet us at the door when we come home. Sam and I have searched the house and haven't been able to find her. I'm beside myself with worry as to what has happened to her."

CHAPTER FORTY

———

A fierce barking erupted from upstairs. I looked at the ceiling and wondered what Annie and Porkchop were up to. "What could those dogs be barking at?" I headed towards the stairs to find out the answer to my question.

"I can't imagine. I've never heard Annie so upset before," Candie said as she pulled out of Mark's arms. She turned to him. "It sounds like it's coming from our bedroom." They both stood and joined me.

When we reached the second flood and walked into Candie and Mark's bedroom, I spied Porkchop and Annie standing in front of their closet door, barking as if their lives were in danger. "Porkie, what's got you so upset? Everything is okay." I walked over to him with my hand outstretched to give him a pat. Instead of wagging his tail in greeting, he snarled at me. I jumped back. He'd never reacted to me in such a manner before.

Candie was greeted in the same way by her sweet Annie.

Mark pointed to the closet. "Something in there has them very upset. You ladies step back while I open the door and find out what it is."

The dogs quieted to a low growl as Mark edged open the door. He started to laugh, a deep, belly rumbling laugh.

"Mark, what's in there that is so funny?" Candie asked, nudging Mark aside. Candie joined in Mark's laughter.

"Okay you two, what's so funny? Don't keep me in suspense."

Candie moved so I could see the object of their humor. *Dixie.* She lay sound asleep, curled up on Mark's fleecy slippers. Porkchop and Annie scooted between us and started to shower her head with doggie kisses.

Candie bent and ran a hand down her cat's back. "Oh, look. Mark. Dixie wanted to be near you while you were at work. The scent of you on your slippers reminds her of you."

Mark laughed. "Yeah, the smell of my stinky feet."

With the mystery of the missing cat solved, levity replaced the gloom from moments before, and we all laughed at Mark's comment. Mark bent and scooped Dixie up into his arms. The cat purred and rubbed her small head against Mark's tie.

"I'd better get back to the office. I kind of left the police chief hanging when I got your phone call." He placed Dixie on the floor, where she promptly weaved herself through his legs.

"Okay, sugar. I'm sorry I panicked. Please forgive me." Candie gave Mark her best sad eyes.

He pulled her into his arms and kissed her. "Nothing to forgive, sweetheart. I care for Dixie as much as you do. I'm thankful she's all right." He turned to me. "Thanks, Sam, for your help in the search for Dixie."

"Anytime, Mark, but really, it was Porkchop and Annie who found her. Umm, you said you were talking to the police chief before you came home. Was it about Ivan's murder?" I prayed they were closer to solving his death.

Candie stepped away from Mark so he could answer me. "Yes, it was."

"Are you any closer to finding who killed him?" I hoped they were, because I was running out of suspects.

Mark shook his head. "I wish I could say the police were, but unfortunately they aren't."

My heart sank. It looked like I was still on the suspect list. Since Drew, Martha, and Sunny all had alibis, it was growing smaller and smaller.

"Thanks. Mark. I guess it was wishful thinking on my part."

"I understand. I'd better go. Candie, see me to the front door."

The three of us traipsed downstairs, followed by a train of pets. Dixie led the procession, followed by Porkchop and Annie.

While Mark and Candie said their goodbyes, I gathered up my black Vera Bradley purse and Porkchop's leash and clipped it on him.

With Mark back off to work and Dixie safe, I said, "I'd better be going, too." I gave Candie a hug goodbye. "You know, I think you can stop worrying about Dixie and Mark getting along. From the way she was loving his slippers and cuddling up to him earlier, your concerns about them getting along are a thing of the past."

A brilliant smile lit up her face. "Thank heavens. All is well in the Parker-Hogan household again."

I laughed and gave her a hug. "Yes, they are. Come on, Porkchop. I think Candie needs the rest of the day to prepare for when her man returns home tonight."

A blush tinted Candie's cheeks.

"Am I right?" I asked.

"Oh, go on. Take Porkchop home and give him some extra kibble for finding Dixie. Tell him it's from his aunt Candie."

I laughed all the way to my Bug.

It was a short drive from Candie's large and stately Victorian to my modest but much-loved brick ranch. It always warmed my heart when I pulled into the driveway of my childhood home. I turned in my seat to find a snoozing Porkchop curled up on the back seat. "Come on, Porkchop. We're home." He continued to softly snore. "Porkie, Aunt Candie says I'm to treat you to a bowl of kibble because you were so helpful in finding Dixie." His ears twitched and one eye opened. I laughed. I knew the word "kibble" would do the trick and wake him up.

I slid out of my car and reached back in for Porkie's leash. I snapped it on and gently lifted my pup out of the car. Once on the ground, he gave himself a full-body shake then followed me up the sidewalk to my front door. "Porkchop, what's this?" Sitting in front of my door was a small square box. The bottom was red and the top white with the word "love" printed all over it. A lovely red bow was tied around the top. "Oh. Porkie, it looks like Hank left me a present. Let's hurry inside to see what he left me." My heart warmed at the thought of Hank leaving me a present like this. Because of Ivan's death, we hadn't spent much time together, but he still showed me how much he loved me. Porkchop began to whine. A growl rumbled up from deep in his throat. He jumped at my legs, causing me to fumble the box.

"Porkchop, now stop that. I almost dropped Hank's present. You're not jealous, are you, that your best bud didn't leave you something, too? You know when he comes over, he will give you a bunch of scratchies." Hank was as fond of my Porkchop as I was of his Nina.

I shoved my house key in the lock, turned the door handle, and nudged it open with my foot. I dropped Porkchop's leash so he could run ahead of me like he usually did, but this time he didn't leave my side as we entered my house. I walked into the living room and tossed my purse on the sofa that sat in front of my fireplace. I smiled, remembering the last time Hank and I cuddled on the sofa in front a roaring fire he had made in the fireplace. More than the fire warmed me that night.

"Okay, first things first. I promised you a bowl of your kibble for helping find Dixie, and then we'll see what Hank left for me." I placed my gift on the dining room table as I walked towards the kitchen.

I reached into the upper cabinet and pulled out a bag of his favorite food then picked up his bone-shaped food bowl from the floor. Porkie's tail usually wagged in anticipation when he heard his food plink into the bowl, but now he sat and looked towards the box sitting on the dining room table. I placed the bowl on the floor, expecting him to chow down, but he stood and walked back into the dining room, where he stood on his two back legs and rested his front paws against a chair at the table. His nose twitched as he whined.

I laughed. "Porkchop, what's the matter? Do you want me to open the box first before you eat? Your curiosity is worse than mine."

I picked up the lovely box and headed back to the living room and settled on the sofa. Porkchop jumped up beside me. There was no note on the outside, but I knew it had to be from Hank. Who else would leave me a present with the word love printed all over the top? "Okay, Porkchop, let's see what Hank has left me. I love being surprised like this." I pulled the ends of the red ribbon that held the lid on to the box. A scream erupted from my throat as I flung the box and its contents onto the floor.

CHAPTER FORTY-ONE

———

Porkchop leapt off the sofa. With a shaking hand, I leaned over and grabbed his collar. "No, Porkie, the rat may be poisoned. I don't want you near it."

My purse still lay on the sofa, so I dug in it for my phone. As I stared at the ugly rat lying on the floor at my feet, I punched in Hank's number. Thankfully, he answered right away. In a shaky voice, I said, "Hank, I need you. Please come over to my house right away."

"Sam, what's the matter?" Phones rang in the background.

I was sure he heard the desperation in my voice. "I'm sorry to bother you at work, but I can't explain it over the phone. You have to see it. Please, come right away."

"You're never a bother. I'll be right there." He hung up, not waiting for any goodbyes from me, not that I was able to formulate any at the moment as I sat staring at the dead rodent lying at my feet. My stomach roiled, looking at its open eyes and mangy fur.

I scooped Porkchop into my arms and hugged him to my shaking body. He squirmed and tried to leap back onto the floor, I was sure to defend me from the rat. I closed my eyes to block out its image before I had to make a dash to the bathroom to empty my stomach. Who would have left such a horrible gift? Was it a message of some type? About what? My brain clicked into overdrive. Duh—it was obvious. I was getting too close to solving the puzzle of who killed Ivan. This was a warning to butt out. I fidgeted on the sofa while waiting for Hank. I wanted to call Candie and tell her what had happened, but a glance at the clock hanging on the wall next to my fireplace told me that Mark would be home soon from work. I didn't want to disturb what I figured would be a romantic evening for them, now that their Dixie and Mark issue was settled.

A screech of tires drew my attention to the front door. Hank must have broken speed records in his drive from the police station when I called him, He had made it to my house in less than five minutes.

 The glass in the windows next to my front door rattled as the door slammed against the wall. Hank burst into the living room. His chest heaved up and down under his Superman tie. Like Mark, he was coatless. His hair stood on end. The wayward brown curl fell over his forehead.

 I held up my hand in a stop motion as he approached the sofa.

 "Sam, what's the matter? You sounded frantic on the phone."

 Porkchop struggled in my arms, but I was afraid to let him go. I didn't want him near the rat. I nodded towards the rodent.

 Hank's crystal-blue eyes widened. "What's that? Did Porkchop drag it into the house? I know dachshunds were bred to be hunters, but he's never done that before, has he? Let me get a broom and dustpan, and I'll get rid of his big kill."

 Tears ran down my cheeks as I shook my head. "No, Hank, he didn't kill it."

 Hank chuckled. "I know you always say your culinary skills aren't the best, but I doubt the rat"—he pointed to the deceased—"sampled any of your food and then expired."

 In spite of the dire situation, his comment made me smile. "No, it wasn't my cooking that caused the rat's demise. He, or maybe it's she, was left as a present on my doorstep."

 "What?" Hank shouted. Anger had replaced the look on his face, where moments before he had made light of my situation. He sank into the wing chair sitting beside the fireplace and pulled a small notebook and pen out of the breast pocket of his shirt. He flipped it open, now in full detective mode. "Sam, tell me everything about finding this so-called present. Don't leave a thing out."

 And I didn't leave a thing out as I relayed it to him, starting with coming home and finding the gift box on my doorstep to opening it up.

 Hank flipped his notebook closed then stood. He slipped his phone out of the back pocket of his slacks and took pictures of the deceased and the box. When he was finished, he said, "I'll be right back. Don't touch a thing." He turned and walked out my front door but was back in minutes, carrying plastic gloves and a bag.

 Porkchop and I watched as he slipped on the gloves then picked up the rat and placed it and the box in the bag.

When he returned to the living room after washing his hands, he sat next to me on the sofa and gathered me into his arms. Gone was the grim look on his face from moments before. It was replaced by the loving and caring man I loved with all my heart. He leaned over and kissed the tip of my nose then leaned back against the back of the sofa. "Sam, you sticking your pretty little nose in Ivan's murder investigation has gotten someone really upset."

I reached up and pushed his wayward curl off his forehead. "I know, but what am I supposed to do? You've been taken off the case. Everyone I can think of who had a grudge against Ivan has an alibi. I don't want orange to be the only color in my wardrobe."

Porkchop nudged his head under Hank's hand. My macho guy obliged him and petted his head.

Hank shook his head, dislodging my efforts of taming his curl. Much to Porkchop's chagrin, Hank placed him on the newly disinfected floor at our feet. He gathered me into his arms and pulled me against his strong chest. "That's not going to happen, Sam. I promise you. You had no reason to want Ivan dead."

"Yeah, tell that to Peters," I mumbled into his chest.

"Believe me, I have," Hank said then leaned down and kissed me. A kiss that wrapped around my heart and wouldn't let go.

When we came up for air, I asked, "Do you want to continue this in a more comfortable setting?"

Hank nodded and stood. He held out his hand to lead me to my bedroom but was interrupted by the ringing of his phone. He grabbed it from the top of the trunk that served as my coffee table and swiped it. After listening a moment, he said, "Yes, okay. I'll be there in a few minutes." He disconnected then cursed under his breath. "I'm sorry, but something has come up at the station, and I have to get back."

I felt like repeating Hank's curse but years of preaching by my Memaw Parker left me with the fear of having my mouth washed out with soap if I ever uttered such words. "I understand. An officer's life isn't always his own."

"Walk me to the door and then lock it behind me. I want to know you're safe when I leave."

I nodded and held his hand as we walked to my front door. Porkchop followed behind us.

Hank drew me into his arms for one last knee-melting kiss before he left. "I'll call when I can. Now lock the door," he said, pulling it closed behind him.

I did as he said then leaned my forehead against the window next to the door and watched the glow of his headlights as he backed his Jeep out of my driveway. Darkness had fallen since he'd arrived at my home. I was about to turn away from the window and retreat back into my living room and spend the rest of the evening snuggling with Porkie on my sofa, when I noticed another glow next to the tree in front of the house across the street. It was a strange light. A small one. It seemed to turn on and off intermittently. Then it hit me. A cigarette. Someone was smoking a cigarette across the street from me. Were they watching my house? Was this the person who left the so-called gift on my doorstep? Should I call Hank back? What would I say—someone across the street is smoking a cigarette? *Don't be silly, Sam,* I chided myself. Do what Hank said, make sure the house is locked up tight, don't answer the door to strangers, and snuggle with Porkchop.

CHAPTER FORTY-TWO

———

Brrr. I shivered and tugged at the afghan I'd thrown over me after I'd settled on the sofa when Hank left. It wouldn't budge. I squinted open an eye and found the reason. Porkchop. He stood on the floor next to the sofa with a corner of the afghan clamped in his mouth, tugging on it.

"All right, all, right. I guess you want to go outside." I swung my legs off of the sofa and grabbed my phone off the end table in case Hank called while I was attending to my dog's demands. Porkie trotted behind me towards the kitchen. I flipped on the overhead light and walked to the back door. Cold air hit me when I opened it for Porkchop to do his nightly business. The backyard was fenced in, so I knew he couldn't wander off. "Darn, Porkie. It's snowed since Hank left. Wait a second, and I'll shovel an area for you." I grabbed the snow shovel I kept next to the back door. I kept it handy to clear a path for my height-challenged pup. Whether he heard me or not, I didn't know. He bounded down the steps barking and growling.

"What's the matter, boy?" I never got an answer to my question. A gloved hand reached in front of me and grabbed the shovel. I glanced up and recognized the owner of the hand. Sunny's husband, Alex. He raised the shovel over my head and was about to hit me with it, when I heard Gladys open her door and call out, "Sam, is everything all right? What's wrong with Porkchop? He's making quite a fuss."

The fear that gripped my tongue loosened for a minute. "Help. Gladys, help. Call Hank. Alex is going to kill me."

Those were the last words I remembered uttering before Alex brought the shovel down on my head.

* * *

My head pounded. What had happened to me? Where was my Porkchop? Was he okay? I said a silent prayer that he was all right. I ran my fingers through my tangled mass of curls and winched from pain when they came in contact with a sticky wetness. I pulled them down in front of my eyes and tried to focus on what I had touched. Through a blurry haze, I saw red covering my fingertips. Blood. My blood.

I glanced around the room and took in my surroundings. I was lying on a musty cot. Cobwebs hung in all four corners of what looked to be a log cabin. The furnishings, a table surrounded by four chairs, sat in the middle of the small room. All looked to be homemade. The stench of cigarette smoke hung in the air. A fire blazed in a wood stove situated in the corner across from me, trying its best to take the chill off the room but failing. I was alone at the moment. My head spun when I tried to push myself up on my elbow and into a sitting position. Since Alex was nowhere in sight, I needed to make my escape or at least think about it. Why had he kidnapped me? The only reason I could figure was he had killed Ivan Kline and I was getting too close to discovering that information.

With a great deal of effort and a pounding head, I managed to swing my legs over the side of the cot and sit up, when the front door of the cabin banged open. Cold air flooded into the cabin. In the doorway stood Alex. Snow covered the knit hat pulled over his stringy hair. He wore a ripped and dirt-streaked coat. His feet were stuffed into scuffed leather boots. Over his shoulders, through the open door, I saw the snow falling at a good rate. He shut the door, walked over to the wood stove, and tossed an armload of logs onto the floor then turn towards me. "Where do you think you're going?"

"Home?" I squeaked out.

He answered me with a maniacal laugh. "I don't think so, Miss Busy Body. You couldn't mind your own business, could you? You had to keep poking your nose into that piece of slime's death. You do know the world is better off without him, right? I did everyone a favor by getting rid of him."

I gulped. "So, you admit to killing him?"

Alex turned back to the wood stove and opened its door. He knelt and threw a log into the fire. "I didn't mean to. I was outside the Center catching a smoke when he came out with Sunny. He started to harass her. He got nasty when she turned down his invitation to go back to his place."

I nodded and instantly regretted it as pain shot through the top of my skull. "I heard she gave him a shove and he fell against the outhouse."

"Yeah, but he didn't take the hint That's when I stepped in to protect my woman, A skillet was lying next to the outhouse, so I bonked him on the head. I warned him if he came near Sunny again, I'd do worse than that."

"Did Sunny know you did this?"

He pulled a pack of cigarettes out of a torn coat pocket. He lit one, inhaled a large drag, and then blew it out. "Nah, she'd gone back inside."

For Drew's sake, I was glad she wasn't a part of Alex's dealings with Ivan. "But why pour the water on him? I imagine he took your warning seriously and wouldn't have bothered Sunny anymore."

A smile spread across Alex's face. He stroked his stubbled chin. "I remembered seeing water bottles inside the door of the Center. I grabbed a few and poured them over Ivan while he was slouched in the outhouse. I told him to cool off his libido. Great touch, don't you think?"

I plucked at the moth-eaten blanket covering the cot. "A touch that led to his death."

Alex chuckled and flicked cigarette ashes onto the floor. From the looks of this cabin, I figured they'd only add to its ambiance. "It's not my fault. People will say he was so drunk, he passed out in the cold and froze to death."

"The authorities might have a different take on your actions. Where are we?" I asked, looking around the room. The cabin was obviously a seasonal place. Probably someone's hunting or fishing getaway. The Adirondacks was dotted with hundreds of these cabins.

"This is a buddy of mine's place. He lets me flop here when I need to."

If it was a buddy of his, I could only imagine what went on here. Sunny had mentioned that the guys he hung out with were into drugs.

"What do you plan to do with me? I won't say a word about what's happened if you'll just take me home." Desperation laced my words. I feared what Alex would do to me if he could so easily dismiss killing a man.

He shrugged his shoulders. "Nothing."

My eyes widened. Hope bubbled up inside me. "What do you mean, nothing? Are you going to take me home?"

Droplets of melting snow flew off his hat as he shook his head. "Nope. You're going to stay here while I head for the border. After I'm settled, I'll send for Sunny and my boy."

Boy, was he living in an alternate universe. Like she'd go to him, especially now that she's found Drew. What little hope I'd had vanished. "But you can't leave me alone here in the woods. How will I get home? I'll freeze to death."

"Not my problem, lady." With that, he turned and opened the door to leave.

"You going somewhere, buddy?"

I smiled, and then shock took over my body. Tears streamed down my face. In the doorway stood my big, handsome boyfriend, Hank. A gun was clutched in his hand, and a fierce scowl spread across his face.

CHAPTER FORTY-THREE

———

Alex's jaw dropped open. He was speechless for only a minute. "What do you think you're doing, bustin' in here like some Rambo-type character? I'm just having a chat with my lady friend here." He turned and pointed a grubby finger at me.

Hank stepped farther into the room, his gun never wavering from Alex. "Let's see what the lady has to say about that. Sam, are you here of your own free will, enjoying an evening chat with this fellow?"

Tears of relief streamed down my cheeks. "He kidnapped me when I let Porkchop outside."

Hank's jaw tightened. "Sam, come over here and stay behind me. Mr. Foxx, I'm arresting you for the kidnapping of Ms. Smanatha Davies. Please turn around."

Alex stepped towards Hank. "She's lying. I did no such thing."

"Hank, he hit me over the head with a snow shovel when I let Porkchop outside after you left. He also told me he killed Ivan. He thought he was doing the world a service by getting rid of him." I could see his body stiffen when he learned that Alex had hit me.

"Stay right where you are, Mr. Foxx, and I repeat, turn around, now."

This time, Alex must have realized by the tone of Hank's voice that he meant business, and he complied with Hank's order to turn around. Hank slipped a pair of handcuffs out of his inside coat pocket then clamped them onto Alex's wrists. He read him his rights. Alex started to blubber like a baby. I guess I should have felt sorry for him, but I didn't. He'd taken another person's life, plus he'd kidnapped me, not to mention given me one heck of a headache from whacking me in the head with that shovel. I prayed he hadn't done anything to Porkchop or he'd be lucky the police got a hold of him first before I did.

The night was suddenly filled with the sound of sirens and the sight of flashing red and blue lights. Backup was here. Within minutes, the small cabin was filled with officers from the Wings Falls Police department. I sat in Hank's Jeep. The car's heater blasted warm air on my cold and shivering body. Once Hank handed Alex over to Joe Peters, he wanted to call an ambulance to take me to the hospital to have my head wound looked after. I declined. Right now, I couldn't handle hours spent in the ER being poked and prodded. My headache was fading, and I was stable on my feet. All I wanted right now was to feel Hank's strong arms around me.

The door to the Jeep opened, and Hank slid into the driver's seat. He reached over and took my hand in his. A worried look clouded his eyes. "Are you sure you're okay?"

I nodded but instantly regretted it. I winced. Apparently, my head wasn't completely pain free, but I still wasn't going to give in to it and go to the ER.

Hank must have noticed my reaction, as he reached over the gearshift and pulled me as close to him as the limited space would allow. "Now I know why people are tempted to commit murder."

I pulled back from his embrace and looked into his crystal-blue eyes. "What do you mean?"

Hank traced a strong finger down my cheek. "When I saw you in that cabin with him and learned he had hurt you, forget the gun I was holding… It was all I could do not to rip him apart with my bare hands." A tear slid down his handsome face. "I love you, Sam, and couldn't live without you."

My heart squeezed in my chest as I reached over and placed my lips on that tear. "Can we leave soon? I want to go home."

Hank straightened in his seat and placed his Jeep in reverse. "Peters can finish up here. It's his investigation anyway."

* * *

The blazing fire in my fireplace lent a warm glow to my living room. Hank and I sat cuddled together on my sofa. Memaw Parker's red and white striped afghan was tucked around us. Porkchop snored softly on his bed in front of the fireplace. He'd been staying with Gladys and Frank. Gladys told me he whined and sat by her door until I arrived home and she brought him over. It took about fifteen minutes of snuggling and scratchies to convince him I was okay. "So, tell me, how did you find me in that cabin? It's a pretty remote area."

Hank chuckled. "I know you don't consider yourself the most techno savvy person, but there are apps for everything nowadays. There's even one for tracing a person's phone. Here, let me show you." He pulled his phone out of the back pocket of his jeans and swiped it. He held it so I could see what he was doing. The location of my house appeared on the phone's screen. "See, that's your phone."

My eyes widened in amazement. "Wow. Thank heavens for modern technology."

"Alex had come up on our radar for Ivan's murder."

I looked up. "How so? I mean, I know he's been a jerk about getting Sunny to come back to him, but murder?"

Hank gently stroked my curls, careful to avoid the nice goose egg that had formed on the left side. "Apparently, Drew Ellis isn't the only one with a smoking habit. Alex has one, too. The crime scene guys found a few butts by the outhouse and had the lab analyze them. Since Alex has been arrested a few times for drug possession, his prints are on file, and we were able to match his to the cigarettes we found. Not only that, but we lifted a thumbprint of his off the 'present' left on your front step."

"He was the one to gift me with the rat?" The image of the rat lying on the floor in front of me still made my stomach queasy.

"Yes," Hank replied.

Porkchop stirred from his position in front of the fireplace. He rose from his bed and trotted over to us. Hank reached down and pulled him up on the sofa with us. I lifted the afghan, and Porkie curled up under it with Hank and me. I smiled, content to be cuddling with the most important men in my life.

* * *

"A lot has happened since last Sunday. Hopefully the outhouse race will go off without any more drama." It had been a week since Ivan Kline had been found in the Loopy Ladies' outhouse. I stood huddled in my down coat and fleece-lined boots next to Candie at the starting line of the postponed outhouse race, waiting for Drew Ellis to shoot the starting pistol for the race to begin. A gentle snow was falling around us. The rest of the Loopy

Ladies were there to cheer on Gladys as she rode to the finish line in our outhouse. We were all very proud of our creation.

Candie rocked the pet carriage holding Dixie and Annie back and forth. "Sugar, it's one week I don't want to repeat. When you told me all about that nasty Alex abducting you, it was all I could do to not march over to the county jail and nail his hide to the wall. The nerve of him messing with one of us Parkers."

I laughed. "I bet he'd rather face a jury than tangle with you." Porkchop and Nina stirred in the pet carriage matching the one holding Candie's fur babies. The weather person had forecast unseasonably cold temperatures for this weekend, so I'd decided to purchase one for Porkchop and Nina to share.

I glanced around the snow-covered field where the race was to be held. People stood three deep waiting to see who this year's winner would be. Five outhouses were lined up at the starting line. "There's quite a crowd gathered for the race. I see Al Gorman, the owner of Al's Fly Shop, has sponsored one." I pointed to the outhouse with leaping trout and bass painted on its sides.

"Yes, and look at the one the Toy Box has entered. Aren't those cute trucks, dolls, and teddy bears painted on it?" Candie nodded to the adorable entry of the town's toy store.

Cheers erupted from the Loopy Ladies gathered around our outhouse. I smiled. It was a repeat of last weekend, minus a dead body.

CHAPTER FORTY-FOUR

———

Hank, Mark, and Brian strode towards us, once again dressed as court pages in tights, tunics, and floppy hats. Frank Gilbert followed behind them wearing his regal purple robe. They marched up to the outhouse where Gladys already sat, resplendent in her queenly cape and a paper crown perched on her curls.

The pages bowed before her. "Good morning, Your Majesty."

Frank stepped forward. He handed Gladys a bouquet of red roses. "For my queen," he said then bent and kissed her on the cheek.

"Is everyone ready for the race to begin?" Drew Ellis shouted over a megaphone.

Cheers and shouts of "Yes!" erupted from the crowd. Those who were to push their respective outhouses to the finish line positioned themselves next to their outhouses.

"Okay, on the count of three, let the race begin," Drew shouted.

The crowd counted along with him. "One, two, three." At three, Drew shot off his gun, the sound causing Porkchop to awaken and bark. Nina slept through it all.

Laughter and cheers followed the outhouses down the racecourse. Tears of laughter streamed down my face as the men slipped and slid to the finish line.

"They won! They won!" Candie grabbed me into a hug and screamed into my ear.

I nodded in agreement, wondering if she'd punctured my eardrum. "Yes, they did."

Frank ran up to the outhouse and helped his queen from her throne. It had been a bumpy ride. I was afraid at times the outhouse might tip over. An unsteady Gladys emerged from the outhouse and gave the crowd a regal wave worthy of the Queen of England. I knew she would recount this day for the rest of her life.

Hank strode up to me. A breeze caught the feather in his slouchy hat, causing it to bounce against his forehead. Porkchop and Nina stood in the pet carriage and barked for attention. Hank obliged them with belly rubs. "The Loopy Ladies can have the outhouse bragging rights for the next year."

"Yes, thanks to you and your fellow court pages. You've made one queen very happy." I pointed to Gladys, who was smiling and reveling in the attention the crowd was showering on her.

Hank shivered. "Yes, and I'm chilled to the bone." He nodded at Porkchop, who lay in the pet stroller with his paws wrapped around the dog bone I'd given him earlier. "Maybe even chilled to the dog bone. Let's get out of this cold, and I'll make the queen of *my* heart very happy."

The look in his eyes was already sending warmth through me. I couldn't wait to see what he had in mind.

ABOUT THE AUTHOR

Syrl Ann Kazlo, a retired teacher, lives in upstate New York with her husband and two very lively dachshunds. Kibbles and Death is the first book in her Samantha Davies Mystery series, featuring Samantha Davies and her lovable dachshund, Porkchop. When not writing Syrl is busy hooking—rug hooking that is—reading, and enjoying her family. She is a member of Sisters in Crime and the Mavens of Mayhem.

Learn more about S.A. Kazlo at:
www.sakazlo.com

Made in United States
Cleveland, OH
24 November 2024

10861003R00116